the rocker

HARLOW LAYNE

the rocker

Join Harlow's mailing list to be the first to know of new releases, free books, sales, and other giveaways!

http://bit.ly/HarlowLayneNL

The moment I saw her, I knew she'd be mine.

The only problem is she's my band's manager, and if we get caught, she loses her job.

I only wanted one night with her. One night to fuck her out of my system and be done with her.

The only problem is after one taste of Pen, I'm addicted. I can't get enough of her, and she's pushing me away.

She says what we had is a lapse in judgement, but I have to disagree. It's the most sane thing I've ever done, and I'll do anything to get her back underneath me, beside me, and to make her mine even if that means ruining what I've worked so hard to build up.

The Rocker by Harlow Layne

Ebook ISBN: 978-1-950044-27-6

Paperback ISBN: 978-1-950044-28-3

Edited by: The Polished Author

Proofreading by: The Polished Author, Amira El Alam

Photographer: Xram Radge

Model: Bruno Chad

pen

"SO WHERE ARE you going that you had to drop me like last week's trash instead of hanging out with my sorry ass and listening to me cry about Brock?" Stella sniffed on the other end of the line, and I felt bad. I wanted to be there for my best friend, but I couldn't control when or where I was sent to work.

"Some small ass college town called Willow Bay. If it makes you feel better, I wish I was there with you. This band is probably going to suck ass and not be worth the gas or the traffic," I grumbled.

"A little," she whispered so quietly I almost didn't catch it through the Bluetooth in my car.

I tapped my fingers on the steering wheel as I tried to come up with something that would lift Stella's spirits. Ever since her husband, or should I say soon to be ex-husband, came to her saying he wanted a divorce and one of the nurses at his practice was pregnant with his child, she'd been having a hard time. Not that I blamed her. But in the long run, I knew she'd be better off. Brock was an asshole on his best day, and my sweet friend didn't deserve to be treated other than the princess she was.

"If Cristiano doesn't have me running someplace else tomorrow night, I promise to hang out with you. We can sit around in our pajamas, do facials and mani-pedis, and watch some cheesy movie on Netflix. How does that sound?"

"Sounds like you'll be miserable," she laughed.

"The things I do for my best friend," I laughed along with her. Once Stella's divorce was final, I knew I'd have to do something epic to break her out of the wall she'd erected once our hometown learned of the demise of her marriage. Living in a small town was hard. I wasn't a fan of everyone knowing my business. I liked being able to sleep with whatever guy floated my fancy and not have the entire town know about it the next day. That's why I lived in LA.

"I'm one lucky bitch to have you in my life. Thank you, Pen, for looking out for me." She let out a defeated breath, and I knew what she was going to say next was going to be powerful. "When the divorce is finalized, I'm moving away from Oasis."

"Do you have any place in mind?" I asked, hoping like hell she said LA, so I'd see her more.

"Not at this moment, but definitely closer to you. I don't want to have traffic or the time of day be the deciding factor on whether or not I see you."

"Hey," my lips turned down at her statement. "I will sit through hours of traffic to be by your side for only a few minutes. But I'm not going to lie. It would be amazing if you moved to LA."

"I think it's time," she paused, and I wondered if she was thinking about her stupid ex. "I'll be ready. Do you want to hear some good news?"

I scoffed. "When do I not want to hear any news from you? Spill," I demanded, taking an off-ramp from the highway. I was close to my assignment for the night and would have to get off the phone just as Stella was getting to the juicy parts.

"I started writing a book about a serial killer in a small town," she blurted out.

"Are you writing about the Scarlett Killer?" I asked, wondering if she was writing about Oasis's very own serial killer.

"No, no. This is just about a wife who discovers her husband is a serial killer. It's kind of therapeutic. I'm basing the husband off of Brock," she giggled.

"That's my girl," I hooted. "I'll be the first in line to buy a copy."

"Oh, I don't know if I'll ever publish it. It will probably be shit, and no one will ever want to read it."

"I want to read it, and so will everyone else," I told her, knowing whatever she wrote would be amazing. When we were young, Stella used to always come up with the most amazing stories, and I knew this would be no different. "I hate to do this, but I've got to get off the phone. I'm almost at the club."

"It's okay, Pen. I understand, and maybe you'll be surprised, and the band will be amazing. What's their name again?"

"Crimson Heat," I answered her. It was a good name, but that didn't mean anything. The last three bands Cristiano sent me to see were trash. I wondered how he found out about them and why he was wasting my time on them.

"I bet they're all hot," she giggled.

"Maybe, but if they're even half as bad as the last one, I'm leaving after three songs. I'm not wasting my whole night here." My GPS gave me instructions on where to turn next, and I pulled into a small parking lot that was full of college kids. "Okay, I'm here. I'll call you when I'm done if it's not too late."

"Here's to hoping you don't call and that they're fabulous. Bye," she called out in a sing-song voice.

"Bye, Stel." I ended the call and slipped my phone into the back pocket of my skin-tight jeans. I learned long ago; purses are not meant for tightly packed bars and music venues. They were too easily stolen.

Stepping out of my car, I inhaled the air. I could almost smell the water of the bay. Or maybe that was wishful thinking since the air was saturated with the smell of cigarette and marijuana smoke along with stale beer. If the outside was this potent, I knew the inside of the bar would be worse. Oh, the things I suffered through for my job.

Strangely, when I walked inside, the place smelled… nice. Okay, maybe I wouldn't take it as far as saying *nice*, but it didn't reek of cigarettes, smoke, and pot. It was good to know the owner kept the smoking to the outside of the building.

A band was already playing, and they sounded like shit. It was some mix of death metal and rap that made my ears feel as if they were bleeding. If I wasn't on the job, I would have made a beeline for the bar and ordered a shot of tequila just to get me through the next few minutes because I wasn't staying long.

Instead, I moved to lean on the back wall and watched as a few people tried to make the front of the crowd a mosh pit.

The band stopped playing, which was music to my ears. I looked down at my Apple Watch to see it wasn't quite nine o'clock, which was the time Crimson Heat was supposed to come on and play. Maybe they went on early, or maybe Cristiano gave me the wrong time. It wouldn't be the first time for either. Either way, I kicked off the wall and started to head toward the door, ready to leave, when a raspy voice spoke.

Slowly, like I was in a slow-motion movie, I turned my head and saw a dark god on stage. He was clad in all black from his black motorcycle boots, black jeans with holes in them, up to his shirt and leather jacket.

I stood dumbfounded as he took off his jacket and threw it off to the side. I wasn't one to be easily turned on, but damn. There was something about the way his muscles rippled that nearly had me panting. I didn't care who he was. I was going to stand there and listen to every word he said and watch every minute detail his body made.

"Good evening, Willow Bay," he shouted, a lazy smile growing on his too-good-looking-to-be-true face. It was like he'd been brought straight out of my wildest fantasies with dark hair with a little bit of curl to it. Eyes so dark you couldn't tell if they were brown or black, but from the aura he gave off, you'd expect them to be black like his soul. I knew the scruff on his jaw would feel delicious between my thighs. Olive skin that stretched over tight muscles that I wanted to touch and lick every inch of. "We're Crimson Heat, and we're going to be here for the next hour. If you know the words, we'd love you to sing along with us."

Leaning back so that I didn't fall down while I stood in a trance, I watched as the singer made eye contact with multiple people in the crowd as he moved around with the grace of a fallen angel.

"I'm Walker. Over here," he pointed to his right to a blond with tattoos covering his arms. "This is Cross, our lead guitarist." Cross flashed a white smile and played a rift that I was sure had wet the panties of at least half the girls in the room. "Greer," he pointed to the other side of the stage to a man who flashed us his silvery-gray eyes. He looked pissed and someone I didn't want to meet in an alley. "He plays rhythm, and last but certainly not least, is Kenton back there on the drums."

Kenton looked up and waved a drumstick. His brown hair that was too long on top flopped into his eyes, and he shook his head to get it out. Even this far away, I could see he had these big, brown puppy dog eyes that I bet made all the girls fall to their knees for him.

Walker's face went from a smirk to serious in a nanosecond. It was like a switch had been turned on inside him. "Our first song tonight is one of the first songs I ever wrote after losing someone very close to me. I hope you like it."

You were my savior.
My everything.
Until you were nothing.
Now I'm lost with no one to find me.
I'm spinning out.
Losing what little of myself is left.
And no one notices.

WALKER'S WORDS WERE HAUNTING. If he wasn't standing right in front of me, I would have been worried about the man who was singing. He sounded like he'd given up on life. Every person in the room could feel the heartbreak he'd experienced with each word he sang. When he sang the last lyric of the song, Walker had his eyes closed. His chest rose up and down as he took a deep breath, and then his dark eyes popped open.

Right there, in that moment, I knew I was in trouble. In one instance, I wanted to fix the damaged boy that stood on stage, and in the other, I wanted to rip off his clothes and maul him.

Neither would be possible when we signed them because I knew after hearing one song, we were going to sign them to Titan Records. There was no doubt about it. I would fight to my last breath to get them a deal because I knew deep down in my bones, one day, Crimson Heat was going to be playing on every radio station all over the world, and I wanted to be a part of it.

Knowing all that, I knew I had to rein in any and all thoughts of being anything other than the professional I was and doing my job.

Which was too bad because Walker was one damn fine male specimen, and I wanted a peek at what was underneath all those dark clothes.

CHAPTER TWO

walker

"THAT'S IT FOR US TONIGHT," I yelled into the microphone. "Next weekend, we'll be down in Oceanside if any of you want to join us. Until next time." I bowed to the crowd and followed the guy's off stage.

"We were fucking epic tonight," Cross clapped his hand on my shoulder and started to bounce up and down.

"Fuck yeah, we were," Kenton called over his shoulder with a goofy smile on his face.

Greer was his usual grumpy self and just kept going, walking down to the back room that we liked to call the green room, but it was barely more than a storage closet. I wasn't sure why we didn't just leave and head back to the house we all shared.

Cross grabbed a water bottle out of the cooler we brought and downed almost half of it before he put the lid

11

back. "Did you see that hottie that couldn't keep her eyes off you all night?"

I looked around at the guys to see who he was talking to and was met with all eyes on me. "Me?" I pointed to myself.

"Yeah, you, asshole. You know all eyes are on you," Kenton laughed as he slipped on a new t-shirt. That man sweated like a beast when we were up on stage. His shirt was soaked, and he smelled less than favorable.

"Whatever. It's not like any of you have a problem getting laid. Well, maybe Greer, but that's because once he opens his mouth, all the ladies go running."

"Fuck you, asshole. I don't need their groupie asses," he shot back, opening the door.

"That's her," Cross whisper-yelled in my direction.

I looked around Greer to get a good look at her, and I wondered how I didn't notice her at the show. Her hair was a light brownish-blonde that reminded me of caramel, and she had the most gorgeous eyes I'd ever seen in my life. They were the yellow-brown of fine whiskey, and I swore I could have stared at her all night and drank her up. I continued checking her out from her slender neck down to her full breasts, trim waist I wanted to wrap my hands around, and her hips that had my dick standing at attention.

Whoever she was. She was mine.

"Hey," she awkwardly said as Greer towered over her. "Um... do you guys have a few minutes so that I could talk to you?"

"What's this about?" Greer growled down at her.

"I'm Pen Rose from Titan Records," she introduced herself, trying to look around Greer's body and into the room.

"Let her in." Kenton pushed Greer to the side and extended his hand out to the woman who called herself Pen. She took it with a second of hesitation. Kent was a smooth son of a bitch. He'd probably have her eating out of his hand in a matter of seconds.

Cross got up out of the only chair in the room and dusted it off. He patted the arm of the chair and waited until Pen sat down to sit on the arm. He leaned forward, putting his elbow on his knee. "So," he drew the word out. "How did you like the show?"

The room went silent as we all waited for her answer. I swear I don't think any of us even took a breath until her entire face lit up. "That was by far one of the best shows I've ever seen. I'm not going to lie. I thought you guys were going to be trash, but..." She shook her head as she closed her eyes. She hummed as if she was reliving one of the songs we'd played tonight. "You guys have some real talent. I'm going to do everything in my power to get you guys a record deal."

Kenton stumbled back a step, and I swear his eyes fluttered. Was he going to pass out? "Are you for real?"

Reaching over, Pen patted Cross's leg, and I don't know what came over me, but I wanted to chop off that damn leg of his. I didn't want her to touch him or anyone else in the room. "One thousand percent. I'm not saying there won't be work because there will be, but I'm going to make you boys famous. What do you say?"

"I say it's too good to be true. I mean, who are you? Can you even offer us a contract?" Greer said in his asshole tone. I was starting to think it was his everyday tone since it had been a long ass time since he didn't sound like he was pissed off or a raging asshole.

"Not me personally. I have to take it to my boss, but like I said, I'll do everything possible to make this a reality."

"Well, until I see you come at us with a contract in hand, I think you're full of shit," Greer growled out.

"Okay, Greer doesn't speak for the rest of us. He's had something stuck up his ass for a while now, and we're waiting for him to have surgery to get it removed. Until *then*, ignore him." I stood and blocked Greer from her view. If he fucked this up for us, I'd kill him. Having someone from a major record company come backstage was a dream of mine. It brought us one step closer to getting in the studio and laying down tracks and ultimately being a household name. "Why don't we go outside and talk where it's cooler, and the testosterone won't choke you to death?"

"I like the sound of that." She stood and stepped up to me. "One day, you won't be in the closet of a bar but have your very own green room at a sold-out stadium."

I opened the door and let Pen step out before me. When I turned back to the guys, they were all standing there like they were going out back with us. Not a chance in hell was I going to give any of them a chance to fuck this up. I shook my head and closed the door in their faces.

Pen was already striding down the hallway toward the back door. Her ass swayed with each tantalizing step she made, and I couldn't take my eyes off it. It was then I realized I couldn't try to get this chick in my bed and jeopardize our future.

"So, Mr. ..." she looked at me expectantly.

"Pierce. Walker Pierce," I supplied for her, taking a spot against the wall. I watched as the heel of her stilettos wobbled on the gravel.

"Mr. Pierce, why did you want to talk to me out here?" Her eyes raked me up and down, and I wasn't sure if it was my imagination or not, but I swore I saw desire in her eyes. Maybe it was the shadow of the streetlight hitting her whiskey eyes.

It was going to be hard to get my dick in check around

her, but I needed to keep reminding myself my career was more important than one night in the sack.

"I thought it might be more comfortable out here without Greer being an asshole."

She let out a soft giggle. "Oh, so that wasn't just for me?"

"Not just for you. I'm not sure what's going on with him, but he's been an asshole for a good while now." I wasn't sure why I was telling her all of this, but it felt good to open up to someone else besides the guys in the band. They didn't care about feelings unless we were fucking shit up for the group, and Greer was doing the opposite. He was making the best music of his life. "I've asked him about it, but he won't talk about it. I'd press further, but he's playing better than he ever has before."

"He can be an asshole. I don't care," she shrugged. "Eventually everyone is, once fame gets to their heads. At least I can expect it from the get-go." She flipped her long hair over her shoulder and then set her eyes on me. "Who writes your songs?"

"Mostly I do, but occasionally Cross and Kenton get in on it. Why?" I asked, trying to hide the nerves I suddenly felt. What if she hated the songs?

"That's good. Then we won't have to pay anyone to use their songs. Keep up the good work. I'm going to go back to LA tonight and show my boss some of the video I took of you guys tonight and see what he thinks." Pen pulled out her phone and then dug in the back pocket of her jeans until she found a card. "Here's my card with my number on it. I'm giving you this as a show of good faith. Don't use this number unless I call you first."

My brows scrunched up at her words. "Doesn't that defeat the purpose?"

"There's no point in you calling me until you hear from me because if you haven't heard from me, then I've got no news for you. Got it?" She huffed and started to pull her hand back.

Reaching out, I grabbed the card from her and stuffed it in my back pocket.

She put in her code, and her face lit up from the screen. Her golden eyes flicked up to meet mine. "Now, what's your number so I can get ahold of you?"

A slow smirk spread across my face, and my chest puffed up, knowing she wanted me. "Are you sure that's why you want my number?"

"Why else would I want it?" She cocked her leg out and placed her hand on her hips. "This is strictly business, Walker. Don't get any ideas in that testosterone-filled head of yours."

"Okay, okay," I held my hands up. "I get it. I couldn't help myself. You're one fine ass chick."

"Give me your phone number before I forget how

17

talented you were tonight, and leave and never come back." Her black fingernail tapped on her phone screen as she waited.

"Alright. I'm sorry," I apologized and rattled off my phone number to her. She may have said it was only business, but I knew it was more. And the thought of my number being in her phone only proved it.

"Great," she flashed a smile. "I'll be in touch." Pen turned to walk away and then turned back to me. I thought for sure she was going to tell me this was all a joke, but those weren't the words that came out of her mouth. "Can you send me the music and lyrics to all of your songs?"

"I guess so." I said it like it was a question when I would do whatever she wanted of me.

"Perfect. My email is on the card. Have a good night." This time when she turned to walk away, Pen didn't look back, no matter how much I wanted her to. I watched her fine ass in her tight jeans make its way down the side of the building and didn't look up until it was firmly planted inside her white Audi TTS coupe.

When I turned to the back door, both Cross and Kenton were standing there with stupid ass grins on their faces.

Kenton cracked up as he stepped outside. "You've got it bad."

"Shut up, asshole. There's nothing wrong with looking

at a fine ass woman." I shrugged and started walking to where we parked earlier.

"Don't leave us hanging, douchebag. Tell us what she said," Cross yelled as I straddled my bike.

"Fine." I sat my helmet between my legs and waited until they reached me. I told them what little Pen had said. Yes, I shot the gun, bringing her out back. I thought it was going to be some long, drawn-out talk where she'd talk contracts and numbers, when all in all, it wasn't much more than a promise.

"Did she really ask for all our music and lyrics?" Kenton's head fell back, and he howled at the sky.

Cross and I laughed at him. Greer was nowhere in sight. Typical.

"I can't believe someone from a huge record label was at our show tonight," Cross said quietly.

"I know, man, me neither. We need to ramp up the practices, and I've already got a new song tickling at the back corner of my brain."

"Awesome, man. Now let's go celebrate," Cross yelled, clapping his hands.

Putting my helmet on, I started to pull away and had to look back at the spot Pen had been parked in. I couldn't help being drawn to it. I had no idea that night would change the course of the rest of our lives.

CHAPTER THREE

pen

2 Weeks Later

CRISTIANO DIDN'T EVEN BOTHER to look at me as he scrolled through his phone. "I'm not sure, Pen. Like I said last time, I thought they'd be... edgier."

I didn't understand Cristiano. He was the one who wanted me to go see Crimson Heat play, and now he'd been pulling this shit for the last two weeks.

"I'm not saying they're one hundred percent ready, but I think I can get them the way we want them. They have so much potential."

He nodded; his eyes flicked up to meet mine for a moment before his phone buzzed in his hand. "Fine, I want weekly reports of their practices, and if I don't see any improvement, then the answer is no. Tomorrow night, I have a show I want you to scout for me. I'll email you the information."

"Thanks. I'll be on the lookout for it." I try to smile as genuinely as possible, but I doubt it's more than a grimace. Cristiano has me at shows every night for the next week all over California. Every band he's sent me to hasn't been worth my time. All except Crimson Heat.

Once I'm in my office, I pull up my calendar and email and then call Walker. It rings and rings, and when I think he isn't going to answer, I hear a jumble of noises and then his raspy voice.

"Hello?"

"Walker, this is Pen from Titan Records."

"Oh, hi, can I call you back in… twenty minutes?" He quietly said, as if he didn't want anyone to hear him.

"If you're too busy," I started because I didn't have time for his games. Either he wanted to be a musician, or he didn't.

"No, no. That's not it. I'm in class. Taking a test," he quickly added. "Can I call you back when I'm finished?"

Holy fucking hell. He was in college? Were the rest of them still in school as well? How young was he? Maybe he wasn't serious.

"Fine," I huffed. My irritation at the whole experience

was rising. I'd been championing for them for the last two weeks, and now I wasn't sure if this was important to them. For fucks sake, they were children.

"Thank you. It won't be long." He hung up, leaving me reeling. What the fuck was I doing? I was staking my career on this band while I had the hots for the lead singer only to find out he's still in school. Walker definitely looked older than whatever age he was. Never once did it cross my mind that he, nor the rest of them could still be in school. I took them to be at least twenty-five which was still way too young for my ass.

Why couldn't I stop thinking about his damn raspy voice or the way his dark eyes took me in when we were outside of the bar? Maybe it was because it had been a few months since my last hookup. That had to be it. I'd find some guy at one of the shows I had to go to this week and fuck Walker out of my system. Then I'd finally be able to think straight.

Cristiano's email pinged in my inbox. I added it to my ever-growing calendar. I swear it was like he was on a mission to make sure I didn't have a life outside of work. I barely got to spend any time with my best friend, and she needed me as she traversed the world as a newly single and scorned woman.

How was I supposed to watch Crimson Heat practice, go to all of these shows, and see Stella? Maybe I could convince her to come stay with me, and she could go to some of the shows with me. It had to be better than sitting at home, so she didn't have to encounter anyone in our hometown. If I ever saw Brock again, I'd kick his ass for hurting my best friend. It was bad enough she put him through medical school, and once he got successful, he wanted to kick her to the curb, but to also get someone he was working with pregnant after trying for years with Stella was the icing on the shit cake.

My phone rang, and when I looked at it, it was Walker. I didn't want to answer. I was in a shit mood now, but I needed to suck it up and do what needed to be done.

"Hello— "

"I'm so sorry, I couldn't talk before," he rushed out.

"If I knew you were in school, I would have considered the time. Is the rest of the band in school?"

"No, just me. They all either dropped out or graduated."

Good to know. Walker was the biggest talent of the band. Without his voice, they'd be nothing, so if he didn't want this, I wasn't going to waste my time.

I needed answers, and I needed them now. "Are you going to want to put your music career on hold until you graduate?"

"Fuck no," he laughed. It was low and rumbly and sent tingles down my spine. "I want this band more than anything. If you told me to drop out today if Crimson Heat had a chance, I would."

Good to know.

"Well, I haven't convinced my boss of your talents quite yet, but he's given me the go-ahead to be at your practices and report back to him weekly. I have two months for him to see what I see in you. The only problem is he's keeping me busy scouting other bands, and Willow Bay is a three-hour drive with traffic."

"Fuck," he growled. "We'll rearrange our practices for you. You just tell us when."

I liked his dedication.

"Do you have practice tonight?" I asked, hoping I didn't regret eating up the one free night I had for the entire week.

"We were going to practice this afternoon, but we can change it to later. Whatever time works for you."

I looked at my watch and saw it was just after two. If I left now, I could be there by five or a little after.

"How about five?"

"Done," he answered back quickly. The excitement in his voice was palpable.

"Text me the address where you practice, and I'll be there around five. Don't make me regret this, Walker."

"I won't. I promise you," he vowed, and for some reason, I believed him.

I⟶ was bordering on six o'clock by the time I rolled up to an old, beat-up house that was far away from civilization, which seemed to be a good thing since I could feel their music from inside my car.

My Chuck Taylor's hit the uneven pavement and carried me toward the music. Even here, they sounded good. I knew I was right about pursuing them. I just had to prove it to everyone else.

I wasn't sure if I should go to the front door since it was clear they were in the garage or if I should knock on the garage. My choice was made for me when the garage door slowly started to rise. I was met with four sets of eyes. Three of them were lit up like I was their favorite present, and the other darted away the second we made eye contact. I really hoped Greer wouldn't become a problem. It wasn't good that he seemed to already hate me.

"You made it," Walker stepped out to greet me.

"Yeah, I'm sorry it took me longer than I expected. I kept getting stopped as I was trying to leave the office, and then the traffic was bad." I gave them all an apologetic look.

"You could have called," Greer muttered under his breath.

I ignored him and moved to sit on a ratty old couch, which I really hoped none of them had hooked up on. From the looks of it, it wouldn't surprise me.

"I got all the music you sent me, and I have to say if you wanted to, you could make a career out of songwriting. They're all good. Extraordinary even."

Walker perked up, and a light shade of pink colored his cheeks. "Really?"

Leaning forward, I rested my arms along the tops of my legs. "One thing you'll soon learn about me is I don't lie. I'm always going to give it to you straight. There's no point in sugar-coating anything in this business. If I do that, it cheapens our relationship. I want you to be able to trust me."

"That's what we want as well," Cross spoke up from his stool across the garage.

"It was hard for me to pick my top three, but I did, and these are the ones I want you to focus on for me to bring back to Cristiano. He's got me booked all over the state, so I won't be able to come to any other practices for at least a week."

Kenton tilted his head to the side, and his big brown eyes bored into mine. "Does he want you to fail?"

"It feels that way, but I'm not sure why." He was the one who sent me out to scout, and it looked bad on him that he kept picking horrible bands for me to go see. If he thought he was going to get me fired, he had another thing coming.

Bright blue eyes looked me up and down before Cross spoke. "Did you turn him down?"

I had turned him down when he came on to me. I'd been working at Titan Records for less than a year. I'd come from a small label that was going under and was pretty much starting over until I proved myself.

"Yeah," Cross sighed. "That's why he's doing it. His ego is wounded."

"He can't really expect me to sleep with him, can he? That would make for a horrible work environment," I mused out loud.

"Did you at least tell him you had a boyfriend to soften the blow?" Walker stepped forward but then rocked back on his heels.

"No, because like I said before, I don't lie. It's just not how I operate." They all looked at me like I was naïve, but I didn't care. I wasn't going to take advice from them. "Let's get back on track here. Unfortunately for you, my time is limited. We have two months to prove you're the next up-and-coming band. Let's start with..." I scrolled through the notes I'd made on my phone. All of their songs were good, but I needed to find the right one to introduce the world to them. "Stay. I think this one has the potential to be your first single."

When I looked up, all of the guys were staring at me with awe on their faces. I knew right then and there; they'd do whatever I asked of them to make them the best damn band in the world.

"Well, what are you waiting for?" I leaned back on the couch and felt a spring pop, but I didn't care. This was what I lived for, and it was time I proved myself to Titan.

"Give us a minute. This all just became very real for us." Walker said as the biggest smile started to spread across his face. He looked to each and every one of his bandmates and then finally to me. "This is unbelievable. Is this how it normally works?"

I shook my head. "Not normally, but I pushed for you guys. If I can't show him what I see in you by the end of two months, I may be out of a job." Fuck, that would suck. I didn't want to have to start over. Again.

Walker looked to me with so much conviction I had no other choice but to believe him. "We won't let you down." One by one, they each said the words—even Greer. And I believed them.

"Show me what you've got."

CHAPTER FOUR

walker

2 Weeks Later

OPENING MY EYES, my gaze was instantly drawn to Pen, who sat off to the side on our old couch. She had a dreamy look on her face. While we had fans, I was only used to the support of my bandmates and Merrick, who'd been my best friend since elementary school. Having a new person believe in Crimson Heat the way she did was a powerful feeling. Every time she sat in this garage, I poured my heart and soul into my words, knowing it could be my last chance to impress her boss.

Pen tapped on her phone, turning off the recording. "That was… that was it, I know it." She jumped to her feet with a wide smile on her face. "If this doesn't convince Cristiano, I don't know what will. Don't be surprised if I have a contract for you the next time you see me."

The guys hooted and hollered in the background, but I couldn't stop staring at Pen. She'd been here almost every day for the last week, pushing us to be better. She was beautiful as always. Each time she came, she was dressed more casually than the time before. I was sure her jeans were still designer, but her heels turned into Chucks, and her silk shirts turned into worn t-shirts. I felt as if she was getting comfortable around us, and I liked that.

She tucked her phone into her back pocket and smiled around the room at each of us. "I'll get out of here and let you guys celebrate."

"I'll walk you out to your car." I held out my arm for her to go first. I hated that she had to leave so soon, but I knew she had a long drive ahead of her. I was surprised she didn't get a hotel room instead of driving back and forth between LA and Willow Bay, but it wasn't my place to ask why she was driving so much. Maybe she did have a boyfriend now. The thought of her driving home to some guy sent a shot of red hot jealousy through me. I didn't like to think of her with any other men but me.

"Oh, you've got to be fucking kidding me," Pen spun around and then shot daggers at her car.

It wasn't until then that I noticed both tires on the driver's side of her car were flat.

"I thought I was going to get to go home and celebrate with some takeout," she pouted. "It's going to be hours before AAA can get out here."

Pen turned to me with her whiskey eyes filled with tears. I was desperate to make her happy like she'd just made us minutes ago. It took all of my strength not to wrap my hand around the side of her neck and pull her mouth to mine.

"I know Willow Bay doesn't have much to offer, but I'll happily take you out to dinner while you wait for AAA."

"That's sweet of you, but it should be me taking all of you out to dinner. Seriously, how do you live here? There's not even a Chinese restaurant."

I shrugged because I didn't have an answer. "I guess because I'm used to it since I grew up here. There are more places in the outlying towns, and they're only a twenty-minute drive. If you hop onto the back of my Harley, I'll take you."

She looked toward the garage and then back at me. "What about the rest of the guys?"

"They can join, but they'll have to provide their own transportation." I started walking over to my motorcycle that sat in front of the garage. "Who wants to go get some dinner with us?" I asked as I grabbed my other helmet for Pen.

"Who's us? I thought Pen was leaving." Cross said, already heading for his car.

"So did I," she sighed. "But I've got two flat tires on my car. I'm calling AAA right now to see when they can get out here to fix them."

"That's some shit luck," Kenton observed. "You didn't do it, did you, Greer?"

Greer rolled his eyes as he packed up his shit. He was the only one who didn't live in the house. "Why the hell would I do that? Count me out. I've got other plans that don't involve you guys."

"Well, fuck you too," Cross shouted as Greer walked down the driveway to his truck. Greer's only response was to flip him off.

"Where are we going?" Cross and Kenton asked at the same time.

"Well, I think Pen was wanting some Chinese food, so I think we're headed to Loganville."

"I don't have to have Chinese," Pen spoke up from beside me. "I was merely pointing out that you don't have a Chinese restaurant here. If everyone else wants something different, I'm fine with that."

"Well, we rarely go out of town to eat, so I'm tired of the few places we have here. I'm down for whatever." Kenton's eyes widened. "Is this our celebratory dinner?"

"Why don't you guys hold off on the celebration until after I bring you a contract. Once I have one in hand, I'll have you all come to LA to sign, and then I'll take you out."

"Hitting LA would be pretty sweet," Cross chimed in. "We can all ride in my car," he suggested.

Kenton and I both backed away. "That's okay. I don't think Pen wants to have to get a tetanus shot from riding in your car. You can ride with me," Cross said. "It's only a two-seater, though. Sorry." Although, he didn't look sorry at all. "Unless you want us all to ride together."

"No, that's okay," Pen grimaced. She had no idea what she was getting out of. Kenton's car was disgusting with a capital D. "It's a nice night, so I'll ride with Walker."

Fuck, yeah, she wanted to ride with me.

"Here." I handed her my spare helmet. I watched as she pulled her long hair into a low ponytail and then placed the helmet on her head. I took the straps from her and secured them.

"Please tell me you're not some type of kamikaze driver, and I need to fear for my life." She leaned in and looked over to where Kenton and Cross were getting in Cross's car. "I've never been on a motorcycle before."

"Oh, then you're in for a treat." I finished tightening

the straps. "I promise not to do anything... too crazy."

Pen slapped my stomach with the back of her hand. She looked down and stared as if she could see through my shirt and straight to my abs. "How about nothing crazy at all?"

"Where's the fun in that? I promise to start off gently." I held my hand out and helped her get onto the back of my bike. Pen was the first girl to get on my bike since my girlfriend back in high school. It was strange to think of Mara at a time like this. I hadn't thought about her in years, and all of a sudden, she popped into my head. Pen was nothing like my ex. She worked for the label, so technically she was my boss. Nothing more.

I got on my bike, and Pen immediately wrapped her arms tightly around me. She felt so damn good with her body hugging mine from behind.

I kicked my motorcycle to life, and Pen plastered her body to mine, not leaving any space between us. The feel of her full tits pressed to my back, and the heat of her pussy had me hard in a nanosecond.

Grabbing her hands, I linked them together and placed them low on my stomach. Were her hands fine where they were? Yes, but I wanted her touching as close to my cock as possible, even if riding with a raging hard-on was a bad idea and horribly uncomfortable.

"Hang out tight," I yelled as I took off down the drive.

CHAPTER FIVE

pen

"SO, you don't like small-town living," Kenton asked from across the table, his usual goofy grin plastered on his face.

"Nope, been there and done that. I'm much happier living in a city that never sleeps, and no one knows me." I plopped a piece of spicy chicken into my mouth with my chopsticks and chewed happily. "I bet you don't even have food delivery in Willow Bay."

Cross nodded, dipping a dumpling in sauce. "You'd be right about that, but it's kind of nice being able to walk almost everywhere in town."

"Well, I hope you like life on the road because if you sign a contract, that's what your life is going to look like. You'll be living out of your suitcase and on a cramped bus."

"I'm so fucking ready for it," Kenton slapped the table with excitement.

Turning to Walker, I asked. "What about you? Are you ready to leave the college world behind?"

His dark eyes scanned my face, looking for something for a long minute before he spoke. "I've never been more ready for anything in my life. Where will you be on this journey?"

Setting down my chopsticks, I looked at the three guys who were giving me their undivided attention. "I can't say. I might be sent to scout more bands or maybe work in the studio with another band. Hell, I could be sent out on the road to manage someone. My work life is in the hands of others."

Dropping his fork, Kenton looked down at his food and then back to me. "Can we ask for you?"

"You can try," I shrugged. "I don't know if it will do any good." I did want to stay with Crimson Heat. I'd been working with them from the beginning, and it would be nice to see them through to the end.

"Well, if you get us a contract, we'll negotiate to have you as our manager." Kenton smiled as he sat across from me.

"Are you sure that's what you want?" Inside I was jumping for joy that they wanted me as their manager, and they didn't see me as a stepping stone to the next part of their journey. "I thought you didn't like my ballbuster ways. If I'm your manager, I'm going to make you work. Hard."

Walker's leg tapped mine underneath the table. "Nope, you're stuck with us."

"What do you say we get out of here?" I suggested. "I'm sure you guys have better things to do than hang out with me." I'd seen the variety of women who stopped by when I was leaving over the last few weeks, and I had no illusions they were there for the music based on their scantily clad bodies.

The boys stood quickly, obviously ready to get back to their regularly scheduled lives. Walker stood to the side and waited for me to scooch across the seat. "Do you think AAA has come yet?"

I pulled my phone out of my purse and looked to see if I had missed any calls. There were a few missed text messages from work and Stella, but nothing about getting my flat tires fixed. "Hopefully. I've only used them once, so I'm not really sure about the protocol. I hope so because it's going to be late by the time I get home."

Fuck, I sounded old, but I wasn't some twenty-year-old spring chicken like these guys.

We head outside, and I let Walker help me with my helmet again. I'd never been on a motorcycle until earlier, and while I was scared out of my mind, it was strangely exhilarating. I loved the feel of the wind in my face and the way the motorcycle vibrated beneath me. Most of all, I loved the feel of Walker's tight abs underneath my hands and the way they'd contract every time I moved my touch.

Walker got on first this time and kick-started the bike. The hum of the bike already had me excited to get back on. I knew I shouldn't be feeling this way. Not about a boy who was sixteen years younger than me and who I was working with, but I couldn't help it. There was something about his confidence that I found so damn sexy, and no other man had ever looked at me the way he did. It was probably because he was a horny twenty-one-year-old and had nothing to do with me. While I thought it was a special look only for me, it was possible he looked at every available female in his vicinity the same way.

He held his hand out, and I immediately took it. Walker pulled me close. Once I was only inches away from him, his brows furrowed as he asked. "Why are you looking at me like that?"

"Like what?" I really didn't know what look had been on my face. I only hoped I wasn't giving away my mix of emotions for him.

"I don't know. If I knew, I wouldn't have asked." His hold on my hand tightened. "Hop on."

I did as instructed, only this time I didn't press myself against his back like my life depended on it. No, I needed to be professional, and this was so far from what co-workers should be doing together.

A startling thought came to me. If I had gotten pregnant in high school, Walker could be my child. The notion made me sick to my stomach, and I tried to keep the Chinese I'd just consumed down. Maybe this was what I needed to keep the line written in the sand. Walker wasn't the one for me. He wasn't even available as a one-night stand. No, Walker Pierce was just a boy I was crazy attracted to but could do nothing about.

As if he knew I was thinking about him, Walker looked over his shoulder at me. I was sure I looked like a crazy person with my ponytail whipping in the wind and a smile that was so big it would be categorized as psychotic, but I didn't care. I'd learned something tonight. I liked riding on the back of a Harley.

He sped up, and soon we were flying up and down hills like they were our own private roller coaster, giving my stomach a run for its money. I laughed, holding onto him tighter as he took a curve without slowing down. "You're crazy," I yelled, but I wasn't sure if he could hear me with how loud the wind and the bike were. If he did hear me, it only spurred him on. Walker went faster. The wind pulled at my clothes, and a chill started to set in, but I wouldn't have it any other way. Who knew the next time I'd have this kind of fun again, if ever?

I hugged myself closer to Walker. My chest was to his warm, broad back, my legs on the outside of his thick thighs, and I gripped his belt loops.

Far too soon, Walker pulled up in front of his house, and I was sad our time was over. I could have stayed on the back of his bike with my body wrapped around his for the rest of the night. I didn't think about whether my tires were fixed or about getting back home. My only thoughts were of feeling carefree as we zipped down the road.

Even though Walker was young, he was surprisingly a gentleman. I couldn't remember the last time any guy held open a door for me. Each time I had to get on or off his bike, he held out his hand for me to use. He opened the door at the restaurant for me and didn't let any of the guys go through until I was inside.

After helping me off his bike, Walker took out his phone and turned on the flashlight as he walked toward my car. "I hate to tell you this, but they haven't fixed your tires yet." He turned to look at me with his head bent down, still looking at one of my flat tires. His dark hair hung like a curtain over his eyes, and I wanted to push it out of the way and feel if his hair was as soft as it looked. "If you want, you can stay here tonight. I can sleep on the couch, and you can take my bed."

"You don't have to do that. I can…" But what could I do? I could go to a hotel, but that would mean someone would have to drive me, and that seemed pretty rude when he offered to let me stay.

"Stay," he placed his hand on my arm and then quickly removed it as if I'd burned him. "I promise no one will touch you while you're here."

"I'm not worried about anyone doing anything. I can handle myself."

"I'm sure you can," Walker retorted. "Come on. Don't you want to hang out with us and celebrate? We might even have a bottle of wine in the fridge."

Doubtful, and if they did, I was sure it wouldn't be any good.

Putting my hands on my hips, I narrowed my eyes at him. "Do I look like some prissy-ass bitch? I can drink beer or whatever else you got with the best of them."

Walker held his hands up. A slow smirk started across his chiseled face. "Not one bit, but you may have to prove it to the other guys."

"Maybe you guys need to prove yourselves to me," I shot back. I had a feeling I was going to regret staying here tonight, but I wasn't going to back down from a challenge.

We were standing at the front door with Walker unlocking it when Cross and Kenton pulled up.

"Are you hanging out more?" Cross looked to Walker with wide eyes.

"It looks like it. My tires are still flat, and your buddy

here offered to let me stay so I don't have to drive home late at night." It was everything I could do not to laugh as both the guys looked to Walker like he'd lost his ever-loving mind.

"Cool. Cool, um… there might be some other people joining us… soon." Cross bit the inside of his cheek. "We thought tonight was a celebration and invited people over on the way home."

"And you don't want to be seen with me?"

"Oh no, nothing like that, but we might not exactly be on our best behavior." Cross glanced at Kenton and then Walker. "We don't want to do anything to sabotage our chance at a contract."

It was sweet that they were worried. "Unless you do bodily harm to me, yourself, or others, I think we'll be fine. I may be old, but I can hang."

Walker opened the front door, and we all filed inside. In all the times I'd been here for practice, I'd never been inside. It wasn't nearly as bad as I pictured it in my head. With how rundown the outside was, I thought the same would be true for the inside. It wasn't the Taj Mahal, but what little furniture they did have was decent. The most shocking thing was the entire place wasn't littered with beer bottles and pizza boxes.

Was it possible these boys were this clean all the time?

"I know what you're thinking, and no, it doesn't usually

look like this. Kenton's mom was here over the weekend, and she cleaned up the place."

I sat down on the slightly deflated but still comfortable black leather couch. "I was starting to think you boys were too good to be true. Don't worry; I won't think too badly of you. I remember what my place looked like when I was in my twenties."

Kenton reeled back. "Wow, wait a minute. Are you telling me you're not in your twenties?"

"It's sweet of you to think I'm in my twenties, but no." I looked at Walker. "Where's that beer you said you were going to give me?"

"Oh, shit, Pen is going to party with us. Tonight is going to be epic." Cross shot up and clapped his hands. "Four beers, coming right up."

"You're going to regret opening your mouth," Kenton laughed.

"Nah, I'll be fine." I swiveled to look at Walker, who was perched on the other side of the couch, to find him already looking at me. The corners of his mouth were turned down as he stared at me with his fathomless dark eyes. "What?" I mouthed.

"How old are you?"

"Haven't you ever been told it's not polite to ask a lady her age? It's rude," I reprimanded him, evading the question.

"It's not to insult you. You look…" he shrugged and bit down on his thumbnail. "I don't know. All of twenty-seven, maybe twenty-eight, if that. So, tell me, how old are you, really."

"Maybe, just maybe, you'll get me drunk enough to find out." I didn't tell him not to count on it because there was no way in hell I was telling them how old I was.

CHAPTER SIX

walker

PEN TOOK a long swallow of her beer and then laughed at something either Cross or Kenton said. I wasn't sure what was said because I wasn't paying attention to them. I couldn't stop watching Pen. Fuck, she was the most beautiful woman I'd ever seen. It didn't go unnoticed that she clammed up about her age earlier, but I didn't care how old she was. Pen was hot. Hotter than hot. She was smoking, and any guy would be lucky to have her. I would gladly get burned by her flame if she let me.

And there I went again. I was constantly reminding myself that I couldn't touch Pen and that she was off-limits.

I wouldn't be having these thoughts if I had a girl on my lap like Cross and Kenton did. All I could do was keep drinking my beer and watch her as she joked around and laughed with everyone.

Suddenly Cross was standing with a girl draped around his side. "I'm not sure if you'll still be here when I wake up tomorrow," he grinned at her and then down at his girl.

"Probably not, but you'll hear from me as soon as I know something." Pen's eyes darted to the woman who had attached herself to Cross. "Have fun... but be safe."

"You're not telling me anything I don't already know," he laughed, swatting the girl's ass. "Good night, all."

"Good night," I mumbled.

"I think we're going to head that way too," Kenton stood, and his girl nearly fell to the floor.

"The same goes for you. You don't need any *complications* right now." Pen eyed the woman's hand as she rubbed Kenton over his jean-clad dick. Was she afraid Pen was going to steal Ken right out from under her, or was she really that desperate?

That girl right there was why I wasn't a fan of the groupies, and I knew the more successful we became, the worse they would get. It wasn't me they wanted. No, they wanted to be able to say they slept with a rock star, or a singer, or whatever. We were just a notch on their bedposts the same way they were on ours.

Pen looked around the room, sipping her beer. It was at least her third or fourth, and she had to be feeling them by now. I had no idea how many I'd had. I just kept drinking and staring like a creep all night.

"I guess it's just the two of us. Are you tired?" I asked, hoping she'd say yes and no in equal parts. I wanted to spend time with her, just the two of us, but I also knew no good would come of it. I'd only become more obsessed when what I really needed to do was get my mind off her.

Maybe if I screwed her once, she'd be out of my system, and then I could devote all of my time to my music instead of constantly thinking about her and her pink lips that she was constantly licking, making them all shiny and alluring.

Pen shook her head and looked at me. "Are you? I can sleep on the couch if you're tired and watch some TV." She looked to our TV that took up almost the entire wall. "What is it with men and their giant ass TVs?"

I shrugged. I mean, who wanted to watch something on a tiny little screen? "What's with women and their huge ass purses?"

"My purse isn't big," she instantly defended hers. Since I'd known her, Pen had a different purse for each day.

"How many purses do you own?"

"I don't know." Her brows furrowed, and her nose scrunched up in the most adorable way. "Why?"

"Because I only have the one TV, and you probably have at least fifty purses if I had to guess."

Her features fell, and then her whiskey-colored eyes narrowed on me. "How do you know?"

I held up my hands when her nostrils flared. Did she seriously think I had somehow been inside her place and looked? "I'm just guessing. Settle down." I got up to get each of us another beer and grabbed the remote as I came back into the room. I sat down next to Pen, where I'd wanted to sit all night. "You've had a different purse with you every time you've come to our practices. I was seriously just guessing."

She took the beer, not taking her eyes off me for a long minute. Finally, she nodded and then finished off her other beer.

"If you're not tired, what do you say we watch a movie?" I nodded down the hall. "Trust me when I say we'll want some sort of noise happening, and soon."

Her nose scrunched up again. "I'm sorry you have to listen to that on the regular, or maybe you don't because you have your own girl with you." Her mouth formed an 'O', and then she covered her mouth with her hand. "Did I cockblock you tonight? If I did, I'm sorry."

"Don't worry about it. I'm right where I want to be. And normally, I don't have to hear them because my room is on the other side of the house."

"Oh," Pen jumped up and then swayed a little on her feet. "Do you have a TV in your room? We can go in there to watch something." She looked down the hall to the other bedrooms. "I don't really want to hear them having sex. I feel like we're not at that point in our relationship."

I stood and ushered her toward my room. It probably wasn't a good idea to have her in my space where I could obsess over her more than I already did, but it was too late now. "Is there a point in any relationship where you're okay listening to someone having sex?"

Pen sat on my bed and leaned forward with her elbows on her knees as she took in my room. "I'm guessing Kenton's mom didn't clean your room?"

"Nope, it's off-limits to her and everyone else. They all know to stay out of my space."

"Oh, should I not be in here?" She made a move to get up, but I sat down beside her and pressed my hand to her leg. I instantly wondered how soft her skin was under those jeans.

"Stay. If I didn't want you in here, I wouldn't have offered you my bed."

She pushed her hair over her shoulder, and I got hit with the smell of citrus. I couldn't quite place if it was orange or something else. Whatever it was, I loved the smell, and I knew my bed would smell like her for days. The urge to bury my nose in her hair was strong, but I managed to keep myself under control.

"Is Netflix okay? We don't have any of the movie channels or anything. Actually, we don't even have cable since we're usually busy practicing." Or other things I didn't mention to her. Sex was definitely a strong component of our lives, but she didn't need to know about that.

"That's fine with me. I don't have anything but a few streaming services at my place either since I'm rarely home and rarely watch TV. Now my best friend, on the other hand, always has all the movie channels, so if I want to watch something, I do it with her.

"What's her name?" I immediately chastised myself. I didn't need to know this information. It only made us seem closer, which was something that couldn't happen.

"Stella," she pursed her lips. "She's going through a divorce right now, and it's hard on her." Pen pulled out her phone and frowned. "I'm surprised she hasn't called me yet tonight."

"Maybe she figured you were busy," I offered, hoping she wouldn't start worrying about her friend.

"Yeah, you're probably right." She put her phone down. "I'll call her in the morning on my way home and check in with her."

"You're a good friend."

"I try," she shrugged. "Do you have anything I could change into to sleep in?"

"Of course, I should have offered. I don't normally…"

"Have girls in here with their clothes on?" Pen laughed, her brows raised. "I guess I'm the first."

She was probably right. I couldn't remember a time when any woman had been in here and not taken her clothes off.

"What's your full name, Pen?" I blurted out. It was something I'd wanted to know since she introduced herself.

Her head cocked to the side as she drew out her name. "Penelope. Why?"

"I don't know. I didn't think your parents named you Pen, but I couldn't be sure. I mean, look at Cross. That's his real name." I wasn't sure why I was rambling on and on. I grabbed the remote from off the floor and turned toward my way-too-big-for-my-room TV, and clicked it on.

Instantly the sound of moans filled the room. I fumbled with the remote trying to turn it off, but Pen took the remote from me and turned the sound down. Most noticeably, she didn't turn the porn off. Instead, she scooted up to the top of the bed and made herself comfortable.

Looking down her body at me, Pen noticed me staring at her for the first time tonight and smiled. "Is this what Netflix is playing nowadays?"

"If it is, I need to tune in more often. This is quality stuff." I didn't know what was playing. I couldn't take my eyes off Pen as she kept her eyes glued to the X-rated show playing on my television.

Her eyes flicked to me and then back to the low moans of a woman. "This is all kinds of wrong, but it's been too long, and I'm horny as hell."

I watched transfixed as Pen unbuttoned her jeans and slipped them down her hips and toned legs that I was finally getting a firsthand look at from the light of the television. If the power had gone out at that moment, I would have gone on a killing spree. I needed to see everything she was doing.

Kicking off her jeans, she settled back down and slipped her hand inside the silky black underwear she had on. The moment her fingers started to move, I nearly died.

"Can I join you?" I asked so quietly I wasn't sure she heard me. I wasn't sure I wanted her to hear me either. What if it broke her out of the trance she was in? I rubbed my aching cock through my jeans and groaned.

The only indication she gave me it was okay was a curt nod. I had my shirt off and started on my jeans before either one of us could blink.

"Keep your underwear on," she rasped and then let out her own low moan.

If that's how she wanted to play this, I was happy to keep my dick in my pants—for now.

I stayed on my knees with them spread wide, watching

her from above. My hand trailed down my stomach, and I cupped myself through the fabric.

"You have no right to be that young and have a dick that big. Do you even know what to do with that thing?"

My eyes flew from where her hand was moving beneath her panties up to her eyes. Her eyes were darker now, and they were trained straight on my cock.

"Age doesn't matter." I pulled my cock up, so it was laying against my stomach, trapped behind the waistband of my briefs. "And I can assure you; I know how to use it. If you give me a chance, I— "

"No more talking," she pushed up on her knees and knelt before me, her fingers circling her clit—something I wanted so badly to see. Her other hand hovered over my rapidly rising chest.

"You can touch me." I gave her the permission I wished she had given me.

Lightly, she placed her fingers against my skin. The heat from that small touch was like a volcano erupting beneath my skin. Every cell came alive, and I wanted more, needed more of her and her touch. I wanted desperately to lay her down beneath me and sink deep inside. Instead, I sucked in a gasp as her hand slowly trailed down my chest and stopped only an inch from the head of my cock.

The intensity of her touch between her legs ramped

up. Penelope's head fell back, and her eyes closed. "Touch yourself."

"I'd rather you touched me," I said, even as I started stroking myself.

There was something about this moment that was more intense and intimate than I'd ever experienced with another woman before.

A guttural growl slipped from my lips, making Pen's eyes snap open and focus on me touching myself.

I pretended it was her hand on my skin, and I was the one touching her. It was my fingers getting coated in her juices and bringing her pleasure.

"I'm close. Are you close?" She whimpered.

I wasn't, but after hearing how turned on she was in that moment, I was ready to explode.

"Can I taste you?" I begged.

Her movements halted for only a moment before she pulled out her fingers and held them out to me.

I dove down and sucked them into my mouth, swirling my tongue around her tangy digits.

"Fuck, you taste good," I moaned around her fingers, lapping at them with my tongue.

What I wouldn't give to dive between her legs and lick her sweet cunt.

We stayed like that, with her fingers in my mouth, me sucking on them, and our other hands chasing our release.

The only sound in the room was our heavy breathing. I knew Pen was about to come when her body started to shake, and her fingers curled in my mouth.

How I wished it was my fingers sliding in and out, bringing her to release.

Pen's body tensed as she let out the sexiest damn moan I'd ever heard in my life, spurring my own release. I came all over my hand, stomach, and chest.

Letting out a soft sigh, Pen laid down on the bed and looked up at me with sleepy eyes. She looked so damn beautiful in that moment. I didn't know what to think about what we'd just done. I wanted to lean down and kiss her. Tell her how hot it was, but instead, I got off the bed and headed into my ensuite bathroom, where I cleaned the cum off me before I headed back into my room.

I wasn't sure where we stood now. I mean, I just watched her masturbate. There was this strange connection between us now.

Moving around to the other side of the bed, I started to say something to Pen when I noticed she was curled up around my pillow, sound asleep. Little puffs of air escaped her pretty pink lips.

Looking to my bedroom door, I wasn't sure if I should leave and go sleep on the couch or if Pen would mind if I slept next to her. It was only sleep, right?

Lying down next to her, I pulled the blanket up to our

shoulders. Leaning forward, I kissed her forehead and let my lips linger there for a long moment, not knowing when or if I'd ever get my lips on her again.

Our night was simple, refreshing, exhilarating, unlike anything I'd ever experienced, and surprisingly so damn addicting. Now I just had to convince Pen for more.

CHAPTER SEVEN

pen

1 Week Later

A KNOCK on the frame to my office startled me, making me hit send on an email I hadn't meant to send yet. I looked up to find a very annoyed Cristiano standing at my door. "Did you know those boys wouldn't sign their contract unless you were their manager?"

"I had no idea they would demand it." It secretly made me happy that they wanted me around. Being their manager was what I wanted, but I wasn't sure what would happen once they signed or if they'd follow through with their demand to have me as their manager.

"Well, they did. They're coming in tomorrow to finally

sign the damn thing." He narrowed his cold, dead eyes at me. "You better make sure they don't fuck up, or it's your career at stake."

"I won't. I promise."

"I want them in the studio by the end of next week and on tour by the end of the year," he demanded before walking out.

By the end of the year, was he crazy? I had a feeling Cristiano was setting me up to fail, but I wouldn't give him the satisfaction. Crimson Heat would be ready if it was the last thing I did.

Picking up my phone, I dialed Walker's number and waited for him to answer. I couldn't help but think back to the last time I saw him. He was sprawled out in his bed, where I left him without waking him up. He looked so damn young as he slept. He had the face of a child but the body of a Greek god. One I wanted to worship. One I needed to stay away from, which was going to be extremely difficult now that I was their manager.

Was it childish of me to sneak out? Yes, but I wasn't prepared to deal with what happened the night before. I couldn't believe I masturbated in front of him. I wish I could have blamed it on all the beer I'd had, but I couldn't. There was no way I could deny my attraction to Walker, no matter how wrong it was.

"Hey," Walker answered, like I called him all the time. "I've been waiting to hear from you."

"I know, but there was a holdup with the contract. Do you know anything about that?"

"Maybe," he said playfully. I knew he had a sexy ass smirk on his face.

"You didn't have to do that, you know?"

"Yeah, we know, but you were the one who believed in us and did everything you could to get us that contract. We want you to be a part of the band until the end."

I laughed, shaking my head. "You shouldn't be thinking of the end right now. You've got a long, lucrative career ahead of you. One that you might not have had by insisting on me being your manager."

"It's worth it. You're worth it, Penelope." The way he purred my name had my toes curling in my boots.

"Listen, Walker, if you did this because you think it's a sure-fire way to get me into bed with you, you couldn't be more wrong. I can't sleep with you. Not now. Not ever. If I do, I'll lose my job. A job that I love."

"We… I didn't do it to get you into bed." His voice went lower as he got serious. "I already told you why. Your belief in us means everything. Now," his tone changed again back to playful. "I won't deny that I want you because I do, but I won't push you either. I can't imagine what it would feel like to be in your position."

"Thank you. Cristiano informed me that you are coming to sign tomorrow. I'll take you all out to dinner to celebrate and to thank you for making me a part of the band."

"Ah, you don't have to do that."

"I want to. I promised you I'd take you out to celebrate, and I keep my promises."

"Okay," he agreed quickly.

"Okay," I laughed. "I'll see you tomorrow."

"Tomorrow," he rasped out, sending tingles down my spine before hanging up.

How could one single word cause such a reaction?

I knew then that Walker Pierce was going to make my job very difficult.

"WHAT DO you think now that you've officially made it?" I asked the guys from Crimson Heat as I walked out of the conference room.

They each had the biggest smiles I'd ever seen on their faces. Kenton was jumping on the balls of his feet, full of energy. Greer's wasn't so much of a smile, but he wasn't pissed off and seemed to be in a good mood, so I wasn't going to push it. Walker and Cross had their heads together as they whispered back and forth.

"I hope you're not plotting something that's going to get me in trouble the first day I'm officially your manager." I stopped in the middle of the hall and turned around to look at them. "I know I've already said it, but thank you for thinking of me when you didn't have to. It means a lot, and I promise that I won't be a tyrant, nor will I let you down."

Cross looked up and met my eyes. "You're one of us now."

"Now, who's ready to celebrate? I've got reservations for dinner at one of the hottest clubs in all of LA, but we can do whatever you want."

"Sounds perfect," Walker said quietly. He'd been quiet with me since he stepped foot in the building. I guess he finally took to heart there could be nothing between us.

"Good, I've got a limo waiting for you."

At the mention of the limo, they ran down the hall and outside to where a black SUV limo sat waiting. They piled inside, and by the time I was in, they had the sunroof open, drinks in their hands, and a bong had appeared out of nowhere.

I'd only been around them once when they drank and never saw them smoke anything. While it wasn't illegal, I wasn't sure being high tonight was the best idea. I kept my mouth shut, though. I didn't want to be a killjoy. Not tonight, but if anyone made a habit out of it, I'd definitely have to put a stop to it.

The driver used the intercom and asked where we were off to first. I didn't want to dictate the night and wanted them to decide. "Do you want to stop by the house the label rented for you, or are you good to go out now?"

"Let's do dinner because I'm starved, and it's only about to get worse." Kenton laughed as he took a hit.

I nodded with a tight smile. It looked like they weren't going to make my job easy. "To dinner, it is," I informed the driver.

I'd asked all of them to tell me their favorite things to eat in a text last night. The boys were easy meat and potatoes men, so I took them to the best steakhouse in town, where we had melt-in-your-mouth steaks. The moment their plates were cleaned, they were ready to roll and hit the club where I'd reserved a VIP section for them. I knew they'd love the preferential treatment and all the women being in VIP brought. What I didn't expect was how I'd feel seeing women vying for Walker's attention. I knew he wasn't mine, but that didn't stop the green-eyed monster from rearing its ugly head when he paid them any attention.

"Hey, Pen," Cross shouted from a few feet away. I dragged my eyes off the girl who was running her hand down the front of Walker's chest and over to Cross. "Why aren't you drinking?"

Good question, because if I wasn't responsible for keeping them out of trouble, I would no doubt be drinking —a lot—enough to burn the touches of other women out of my brain.

"Can't. I'm on the job." I held out my water to him and gave him an air cheer.

"That's got to suck. You can't let loose for one night," Kenton muttered beside me, or at least that's the way it sounded with the loud beat of the music filling the air.

"I've already done that, remember?"

"Yeah, you were awesome," he chuckled. "Does it bother you to see all these girls— "

"Not at all," I cut him off, not wanting to hear him voice what they all probably knew. "I was young once, and I know boys will be boys."

Leaning forward, Kenton's grin grew. "I still think you're lying to me. There's no way you're in your thirties."

One brow rose as I asked. "Who said I was in my thirties? What if I'm in my forties?"

Which, dear God, would make it a sin for me to be looking or having the thoughts I did about Walker. Although thirty-seven was damn close to that forty mark.

Out of the corner of my eye, because I hadn't stopped watching no matter how hard I tried, I saw Walker move to sit down on the couch closest to me. "There's no fucking way you're in your forties."

"No," I shook my head, unable to hide my smile. It might kill me if they thought I was that old. "I'm not, but it was fun to see the look on their faces when I said I might be."

Walker leaned forward and placed his elbows on his knees. "Don't start playing them like that, or you won't like the payback. They are ruthless when it comes to pranks."

Duly noted. I didn't need all of them trying to prank me. I would be a sitting target unable to come up with anything good to get back at them with.

He leaned forward more. I wasn't sure if it was so I could hear him better or if he wanted to be closer to me. In my head, I wanted it to be the latter no matter how many times I told myself I didn't.

"You know, I heard that if you want people to think you're drinking, but you're not, you order drinks that look like they could be anything." Walker's eyes went to my bottle of water.

I held up my water. "And this can't be anything?"

"Not in the bottle," he shook his head. "Get a cranberry and something, or hell, even a Sprite."

"Why do you care if it looks like I'm drinking or not?"

One shoulder rose nonchalantly. "I don't, but I think if

the guys thought you were drinking, it might make them give you less of a hard time."

"I can handle them, and anyway, I'm not sure how professional it would seem if I looked like I was drinking with you guys."

"Suit yourself," he smirked before getting up and going back over to the group of women who'd previously been throwing themselves at him.

"You know jealousy isn't a very good look on you," Greer gritted out through clenched teeth.

"Why do you care?" Maybe he was jealous that I didn't want him the way I wanted Walker.

"I don't, but I wouldn't bother wasting your time or career on Walker. He's not the boyfriend type of guy." He nodded toward where the man in question was getting felt up by at least three women. "This is only the beginning. If we make it big like you keep promising, you won't even be able to see him with how many women are in front of you."

"You're such a good friend." I didn't even try to hide the sarcasm in my tone.

"I tell it like it is, and I don't want this to be awkward. We're stuck with you now, and if you're off crying in the corner every time he fucks someone, you're going to get dehydrated really fucking quick."

I wasn't sure if Greer was looking out for his friend and

band or if he was being an ass. I knew he wasn't saying it for my benefit.

"I don't plan on this being anything more than professional. With *all* of you." I gave him a pointed look. There would be nothing between me and any of them besides friendship.

Maybe he was hurt that he missed hanging out the night I stayed with them. I didn't know, nor was I going to care.

I stood, and all eyes were suddenly trained on me. "I'm going to hit the little girl's room." Walker's dark eyes met mine, and there was something lurking in there, but what I couldn't say. As he continued to look at me, his brows drew down, and a frown started to form. I gave him what I hoped was a reassuring smile before I got lost in the crowd.

I needed to get my head on straight by the time I got back to our section. It wasn't good that Greer read me so well, and I was stupid enough not to deny his claim. Taking a deep breath, I closed my eyes and tried to find the calm inside me, only I couldn't find it. Inside I was festering with thoughts of girls all over Walker and how I'd have to see him parade them in and out in front of me if—no *when*— they went on tour. It would be pure torture, but maybe it was what I needed. I wasn't a masochist. I'd move on.

What I needed was to find a man that would attend to

all of my needs. Maybe I'd find one when Stella, the girls, and I went on our trip to celebrate her divorce.

First things first, though. I needed to get these boys in the studio to create the best damn music they could make. Only then would I be able to go on vacation. I hoped I'd be over my feelings for Walker by then.

Scratch that. Maybe I needed to find myself a man tonight to put this silly crush to bed once and for all.

With that thought in mind, I headed out of the restroom with only one mission: Get laid and forget about Walker Pierce.

CHAPTER EIGHT

walker

"I THOUGHT this was going to be fun, but this is like the practice from hell," Kenton grumbled from behind his kit.

Cross made his way across the room and threw himself down on one of the two couches in the room. "No shit. How many different ways can we sing the same song? I think we're going to hate our music before we get done recording this album."

"Hey guys," Pen chirped as she came into the room. She was all sunshine and rainbows, something we needed at that moment. She reeled back when she finally got the vibe of the room. "What's going on?"

"We've played Stay about a hundred times today, and that dick in there keeps telling us to do it again and again, and different. It's like he can't make up his damn mind. My fingers are about to start bleeding." Greer rubbed his fingers for emphasis.

"Really?" She sighed and looked through the window. "Let me go have a talk with Wallace and see what I can do."

"Thanks," I muttered. "Oh, hey, Pen." She spun on her heel and faced me. "I ordered you one of those salads that you like for lunch. It should be here soon."

The guys laughed and called me pussywhipped under their breaths, but I wasn't sure how you could be pussywhipped when you weren't getting any.

"Thank you, Walker. That's so sweet. I thought I'd missed out on lunch and was going to have to wait for dinner." She hugged her MacBook close to her chest. "When I get back, I have something to show you guys."

"What is it?" We all shouted in unison.

She shook her laptop and walked backward. "You'll just have to wait and see. First, I need to see what's going on in the control room."

We might not have been able to hear what was going on in the control room, but we could watch. I moved to sit on the couch opposite of Cross and pretended like I could read lips and understand what was being said in there. I had no clue, but I did know that Pen wasn't happy. After ten minutes of back and forth, she stormed out. By the time she reached us, we were all standing, waiting to hear what she had to say.

She looked around the room, and I swore she looked like she wanted to stomp her foot. Her face was red with her lips pursed. "The rest of the day is canceled. Tomorrow you will have someone new producing in the control room. This whole bullshit—" she pointed to the other room. "Has tainted what I wanted to show you. Do you want to get out of here?"

"What about our lunch?" Kenton asked, shoving his hands in his pockets.

"Right, right," she muttered to herself. "Let's go outside and wait for it to arrive. We can eat out there. It's nice outside, and you boys need your vitamin D."

"I think you need some vitamin D," Kenton chuckled, following behind Pen. I slapped him on the back of the head and narrowed my eyes at him.

"Don't think I didn't hear you back there," Pen called out. "And you're not wrong. I do need some D, but first, I need to find the right man for the job."

My steps faltered for a moment. I was the right man for her, even if she didn't realize it. At least not yet. But I wasn't going to push her. I was going to let Pen figure it out on her own, or at least hope she did.

Kenton ran up on Pen and wrapped his arm around her shoulders. "Can I apply for the job?"

Laughing, Pen pushed him away. "In your dreams, Kenny Boy. Find someone your own age."

Pen mentioned age a lot, and it made me wonder if that was what she really was concerned about. Did she think she was too old for me? Because I didn't care how old she was, which was something she had yet to divulge.

By the time we got to the front of Titan Records, our lunch was sitting at the front desk waiting for us. Pen stopped in front of the bags and spoke to one of the receptionists.

"We're going to be outside having lunch, and we are not to be disturbed." She gave the poor woman a look that let her know there would be hell to pay if we were bothered.

"Damn, Pen. You're one badass bitch when you want to be," Cross hooted, taking the bags from her.

She raised a brow, giving Cross a pointed look. "You just wait until it's turned on you."

"Oh, that's never going to happen. I'm always going to be on your good side." Even though I couldn't see him, I knew Cross had a wicked smile on his face. "I'm always a good boy. The best behaved out of all of us."

I scoffed at his comment. None of us were out getting arrested on the daily, but we weren't angels either.

Pen turned to walk backward with her golden-brown eyes narrowed at all of us. "I don't believe that for a second. Now let's sit down and eat, so my blood pressure can lower just a little bit." She sat down at one of the tables and closed her eyes. I didn't like not being able to see what she was thinking. It was almost like I willed her eyes to open when they popped open and landed on me. "Why didn't you call or message me to let me know he was being difficult?"

"I didn't think there was anything you could do about it." I sat down across from her and watched as Cross unpacked our lunch. "I thought it was part of the process."

"I had him play me the last one, and it sounded good. No, strike that. It was great, and Wallace had no right to keep asking for more from you, especially if they all sounded like that. I requested that Ernie work with you from now on."

Cross stopped what he was doing and looked up at her. "Thanks."

"You don't need to thank me. It's my job." She opened her salad and looked up at us. "Besides today, how are you guys? I'm sorry I've been a little MIA this week, but I had to finish up a few other things before I'm officially your manager."

"That's badass," Kenton hooted before he sat down at the table.

Pen reached across the table and patted his hand. "It

really is. I can assure you I've been a manager before, just not with Titan."

Pulling my lunch order in front of me, I cocked my head to the side as I took in her words. "So, you haven't always been with Titan?"

Stabbing at her food, Pen nodded. "I was at a smaller company and realized they were never going to use me to my true potential. So essentially, I had to start over here and prove myself."

"Well, it looks like you've done that and more. You know if you want to blow off some steam, you can come to the house they got for us and hang out with us by the pool." Now that I thought about it, I realized it probably wasn't just a nobody who got the house for us. "Did you have anything to do with getting us that house?"

The house was what we all dreamed our houses would be like when our band finally made it big. It was a mansion. We each pretty much had our own wing, there was a huge ass kitchen that was going to waste since none of us knew how to cook, and there was a sick ass pool with a whole grotto thing going on. Cross and Kenton were inviting over any woman they saw on the street, trying to recreate the Playboy mansion.

She chewed her food, nodding. "I may have had something to do with it. Do you like it?"

"Like it? We fucking love it. I want to buy it someday," Kenton banged his hands on the table excitedly.

"And one day, you will. For now, keep dreaming about it when you have an asshole like Wallace giving you a hard time."

"What's his deal anyway?" I asked. Either Pen had blinders on where we were concerned, and we weren't all that, or there was something else going on.

She looked off to the side as she drank from her water bottle. "Wallace was supposed to be on vacation for the next two weeks, but it was canceled. He was told that if he went on the vacation that he'd been planning for a year, he'd be fired."

"Fuck, that's harsh." Cross flipped his phone end over end.

"But that's not a good excuse to give us a hard time. Maybe if he wasn't being an asshole, we'd finish recording early, and he could go on his vacation." Greer huffed and then chomped down on his burger.

"There's no good excuse as to why he was being an ass. That's why he's being replaced." She hung her head, biting her lower lip. "I should have been there."

"Hey," I enveloped her tiny hand in mine, and our eyes met. "You were doing what you needed to, so you can take care of us like you're doing now. Not everything can be easy. Otherwise, it wouldn't be worth it."

Pen's phone pinged, and she looked down at the message.

"Hey, do you want to play hacky sack while they finish eating?" Cross asked the guys.

I looked down at my uneaten food, realizing I'd been too busy watching Penelope.

"Let's go." Kenton grabbed up their trash and threw it away in a nearby trashcan. I watched as they moved further away to play.

"I didn't know people still played that. I was never any good at it. I was always lucky if I hit it once with my foot." She looked at them playing and laughed. "Walker, why are you being so nice to me?"

Leaning forward on my elbows, I searched her golden eyes. "Why wouldn't I be nice to you?"

"I don't know. Maybe because I skipped out on you, and I've been putting distance between us since that night. I'm supposed to be the adult, and instead, I've acted like a child. I'm sorry."

"First of all, we're both adults here, and second, I understand the position you're in. I actually have a friend back in Willow Bay who's got the hots for his teacher. He's trying everything in his power to hook up with her."

"And if they get caught, she loses her job, right?" Her eyes widened, giving me a knowing look. I did understand what was at risk for her, and I didn't blame her for keeping as much space between us as possible.

"Yeah, she would," I acknowledged.

"And she might lose her teaching license as well. I can see why she'd have a problem with giving in *if* she's even interested. Plus, she's probably older than him."

There it was again—the age difference.

"I'm going to ask you something, and it's not to offend you or anything like that."

She looked over to where the guys were still playing for a moment and then back to me with a slight downturn of her lips. "Okay, I'm not sure I'm going to like where this is going, but what is it?"

Reaching forward, I hooked my index finger with hers. Her skin was so soft and warm, making me wonder if it felt that way all over. "Not that it matters to me, but how old are you?"

The moment the words were out of my mouth, Pen pulled away. "I'll happily tell you. Then you won't be interested in me anymore, and we can get on with our lives."

Doubtful, but I wouldn't tell her that.

"I'm thirty-seven. Happy?"

"Yeah, because now that it's out there, and I can tell you I don't care that you're thirty-seven or forty or any age. What I do know is my dick gets harder for you than it has for anyone before you. Neither one of us care. The only one that does is you."

"Walker, I…" her mouth opened and closed a few times before her eyes got misty, and she looked down at her food. "Yes, the age difference is a part of it, but it's also because I'd be risking everything for something that will likely fizzle out very quickly."

Fire burned through my veins and settled in my gut. She had no idea how I felt. "On whose end? Because I can tell you right now, I won't be getting tired of you."

"You think your dick won't get tired of me, but I can assure you, it will." She steeled herself, squaring her shoulders before she continued. "And it will get lonely when you're out on the road. Then your dick will get very excited when there are women throwing themselves at you morning, noon, and night."

I stood, pushing off the table, my food forgotten. The only thing that ran through my mind was Penelope's words.

I leaned forward and gritted out the words. "That's not me, and never will be. You don't know me."

"And you don't know me," she stood, placing her hands on the table only inches from mine. "We don't know each other. That's why this is a gamble. Do you really expect me to risk everything on a fling? Because I can tell you I've seen more men than I can count say they're going to be faithful only to crumble once temptation was put in front of them."

I moved as close as I could with the table between us until there were only a couple of inches between us. "Let me show you I'm different."

Her gaze landed on my mouth. As if I couldn't help myself, I licked my suddenly dry lips. "Show me what you've got."

CHAPTER NINE

pen

WALKER WAS SERIOUSLY TRYING to kill me with kindness while simultaneously making me one jealous bitch.

Every night the guys invited me over and threatened to get into trouble if I didn't show up. I wasn't sure if they were joking or not, but I couldn't risk it. They were so close to finishing up the recording of their first album.

While Walker never laid his hands on the women while I was around, I wasn't spending the night to make sure none of them stayed the night. That wasn't my job, and I couldn't risk falling into bed with Walker myself.

Maybe if I found some other man who could treat me with respect like Walker did, he could get me out of thinking about the guy I was supposed to keep out of trouble and make his career. You would think it wouldn't be difficult to find a guy who remembered how you drank your coffee or what you ordered from every place you'd eaten together. Hell, it shouldn't be that hard to find someone who opened doors for you or helped carry your bags.

Going outside to sit by the pool, I pulled out my phone and started swiping through Tinder. The only problem was none of them had dark hair and eyes that reminded me of midnight. None of them had a jaw sharp enough to cut diamonds either. I couldn't hear what they sounded like, but I knew they didn't have that low rasp Walker had. His voice was pure seduction without even trying.

Those dark eyes I was dreaming about appeared in front of me. They held so much kindness in them that I wanted to give in. I mean, what would it hurt if I gave in? If I let temptation take over for one night? Maybe then we'd both get it out of our systems, and we could go on with our lives.

"What are you doing out here by yourself?" He leaned over, and before I could hide what was on my screen, he caught a glimpse. "And why are you looking on Tinder when you've got someone who's very interested right in front of you?

Leaning back in the chair, I brought my phone to my chest before I met his narrowed gaze. "Who says I'm interested in you?"

Turning the chair next to me so he'd be facing me, Walker sat down with a smirk so sexy, I wanted to kiss it right off his smug face. "I see the way you look at me."

"No, you don't," I denied. I hated that I was so damn transparent around him.

"Like right now." He moved forward until our knees were touching. Heat bloomed through my body, and I wanted desperately to disconnect the hurricane that was brewing inside of me. "You're looking at me like you want to devour me."

I jerked my seat back in order to break our connection. "I think you're confusing me with all the women you've been surrounding yourself with."

"Are you jealous?" He asked with a mocking laugh.

Was he fucking kidding me right now?

I stood, backing away from Walker, and didn't stop until my back came into contact with one of the tables that sat around the pool.

"Whoa. No, no, no." Walker stood walking toward me with his hands up in the air, eyes wide. "Pen, no. Don't take it like that. You know I'm into you, and I've been giving you your space. Do I like the idea that you might be jealous? Hell, yeah, I do because that means you feel something for me." With his hand outstretched toward me, Walker's face softened. When I didn't reach out to him,

Walker let his arm fall to the side. "Fine, then tell me why you were on some dating app just now?"

I crossed my arms over my chest and narrowed my eyes at him. Who was Walker to ask me anything? I didn't owe him any answers, and yet, I still answered him.

"Because I thought if I found a guy who could treat me right and give me a few orgasms that my attraction to you might fade altogether."

Walker stepped toward me and picked up my hand. He ran his long fingers over the tips of mine. "Are you not satisfying yourself?"

"I'm woman enough to admit sometimes a girl just needs the real thing."

"And you need a real…" His lips twitched to the side as if he was holding back laughter.

"Dick. I need a penis, preferably a big one inside of me." Now that the words were out of my mouth, I may have overshared on that one.

Tugging on my hand, Walker ran my hand down his taut stomach and along the hard length hidden behind his jeans before I could think or react. When I tried to pull back, he shook his head. "Is this big enough for you?"

He knew it was. There was no way Walker didn't know he was packing an anaconda in his pants. When we masturbated that one night it was dark in the room except for the light coming from the TV, but even in the dim light, I could tell he was huge.

"I can satisfy you in more ways than one." I started to tell him no when he placed his finger over my lips. "I'll be good to you."

And I knew Walker would be good to me. In and out of bed—at least until he got tired of me.

Lacing my fingers with his, I pulled him along with me as I went around the house from the backyard to my car.

"Where are we going?" He asked as he came to walk beside me.

"Don't ask questions. If you don't want to come with me, you can go back inside, and I'll see you on Monday." I kept moving, wondering what Walker would choose to do. When his fingers tightened around mine, I walked faster to my car.

Walker kept true to my request as we got inside my car and drove away from the house where he was staying, heading toward my place. As I pulled into the parking garage, I could see him out of the corner of my eye, looking around curiously.

Pulling into my parking spot, I turned off my car and stepped out. Walker was hot on my heels. He reached out to grab my hand as we walked through the door to the lobby. The second I felt the tips of his fingers touch mine, I pulled away.

Bobby, the doorman, tipped his chin to me. "Have a good evening, Ms. Rose."

"You, too, Bobby." I gave him a wave as we entered the elevator.

The second the doors closed, Walker turned on me. His hot breath feathered against the oversensitive skin of my neck. "Are you embarrassed by me?"

His tongue ran along the shell of my ear. I gasped at the contact, already knowing this was a bad idea. "I don't want you or Bobby to think this is more than what it is."

"And what's that?"

"We're getting this—whatever it is—out of our systems." I pointed back and forth to the two of us, even though I knew he couldn't see it. Walker's lips and tongue were trailing a path down the column of my neck. My pulse was erratic as I whispered. "Plain and simple."

"Speak for yourself. There's nothing plain or simple about the way I want you." One of his hands slipped underneath the hem of my shirt. The heat of his large hand on my stomach had my whole body shaking, and when his hand started to travel north, I thought I might combust.

The doors to the elevator opened with a ding, and we tumbled out all hands and legs. I couldn't wait to get my hands on his body. To feel the way his muscles contracted with each touch.

"Which one is yours?" He rasped, leaning down and running his tongue down the back of my neck, sucking on my skin. He was marking me, and it was the biggest turn-on.

"Last one on the end."

Walker nearly picked me up as he rushed me down the hallway. I pulled out my keys, unlocking my front door. We stepped inside to the lights of LA shining brightly through the floor-to-ceiling windows that wrapped around both sides of the living room and kitchen area.

"That's one hell of a view."

It should be for the kind of money it cost me to buy it. I loved being able to see all of LA from anywhere in my condo.

Turning me around, Walker took off my shirt and started on the button of my jeans. "I want to fuck you out on that balcony of yours."

Kicking off my boots, I lifted his shirt by the hem. He dipped his head, letting me pull it over his head. My hands immediately fell to his torso and ran down the plains of his abs. "Is that where you are choosing to have me for your one and only time?"

Kneeling down in front of me, Walker pulled my jeans down my legs. His calloused hands ran up the outside of my quivering thighs. Running the tip of his nose along the fabric of my already drenched panties, he breathed in and moaned deep in the back of his throat. "Oh, no, my sweet Penny. Once you have my dick, you're not going to be able to stop at just one fuck. You're going to be begging for it over and over again."

As he stood, I pulled down his zipper and wrapped my hands around his impressive and intimidating length. "You're awfully cocky."

"You would know. You've got those soft hands of yours wrapped around me." He jutted his hips into my hands. "Why do your hands feel better than anyone else who's touched my dick?"

I shook my head and lightly laughed at his words. "Maybe if you want this to go any further than my hand on said dick, you shouldn't mention anything about all the other women who've touched it."

"I promise never to mention another woman in your presence again, so long as you keep touching me." Head tipped back, his Adam's apple bobbed with each word. Why was that so damn sexy?

Kicking off his shoes and stepping out of his jeans, Walker picked me up and strode over to the bank of glass. Placing me on my feet, he opened the door and guided me out until my front was pressed into the railing. The chill in the air and the way he was touching me had goosebumps erupting over every inch of skin.

"Fuck, I thought you were beautiful before, but standing here before me right now, you're... exquisite."

Expertly, he divested me of my bra and panties in record time. Soft lips trailed open mouth kisses up my spine and across my shoulder.

I wanted to turn around and put my mouth anywhere and everywhere on his skin, but Walker kept me pinned where I was. He touched me as if he was mapping out each curve and valley of my body.

I moaned and arched my back into his touch. I'd never wanted anything more than his body flush against mine and his erection pressing into the small of my back.

Walker's hands and mouth were everywhere but where I wanted him. I had to give him credit. He was good. He had me so wound up. "I need more," I begged.

"Patience. If this is my only chance to touch your body, then I'm going to take advantage of having you at my mercy."

I turned, looking over my shoulder, and chased his mouth with mine. His arms came around me, cupping my heavy breasts as he licked along the seam of my mouth. "Is this what you want?" He asked only seconds before slipping his tongue inside. He licked and nibbled. His tongue slid against mine, tasting me while rubbing his length along my ass.

When we broke apart, I was panting with need.

"You're diabolical. I'll give you the rest of the weekend if you put me out of my misery and fuck me now."

"I told you you'd beg for me," he chuckled and licked along my bottom lip.

I bit his bottom lip and tugged. Letting go, I smirked up at him. "Shut up and fuck me before I take matters into my own hands."

Knowing I would, he pressed his hand between my shoulder blades with one hand and gripped his cock with the other. "I hope you're wet, baby." Two fingers dipped inside, pumping once before he pulled out. "God, you're fucking soaked for me. You have no idea how much that turns me on."

I groaned with frustration, although I didn't have to wait long. Slapping my legs apart, Walker positioned me exactly the way he wanted with my ass out and on display. In one thrust, he plunged deep inside, filling and stretching me with delicious pain. My hands scrambled for purchase, needing something, anything to keep me in the here and now.

He pulled back until he was so close to leaving me and then slammed back inside. Walker did this over and over again. Punishing my pussy.

I moaned loudly, not caring if my neighbors heard or saw me. All I cared about in that moment was the way

Walker's cock magically hit the spot inside of me very few had ever found before.

"Walker," I gasped his name. "More."

Instead of giving me what I wanted, Walker turned me around. He was a sight. His eyes were black with lust, and his dick was coated in my juices, but it was the way he looked at me like I was the most beautiful thing in the entire world that caught my body on fire. He sat down on the lounger built for two and pulled me down on top of him. Lining himself up at my entrance, I lowered myself until he was fully sheathed inside of me. Dipping his head, Walker took one aching nipple into his mouth as his thumb found my clit and started to rub. With my hands on his shoulders, I rode his large cock like the fate of the world rested in how well I could get us both off.

It didn't take long until I started to come undone around him. With his mouth taking turns torturing and soothing my sensitive nipples and his thumb making furious circles between my legs, I shattered around him. With my head thrown back, I moaned his name over and over again as I rode out my climax.

Walker's hand came around from the back and held onto my shoulders as he held me in place while he thrust up once, twice, and on the third time, he stilled deep inside of me. Letting out a sexy growl, he held me to him and hummed.

After a few minutes of us panting and catching our breath, Walker kissed the side of my neck. He pulled back, lifting his head to look at me with a lazy smile. "Fuck, I think you milked me of everything I had."

I sagged against him, unable to move, let alone think. Walker was right. If sex with him was always like that, I would come begging for more.

Resting his forehead to mine, Walker stared at me for several seconds before he spoke in a quiet, vulnerable voice I'd never heard from him. "Are you going to kick me out now?"

"Not yet. First, I need to see if you can eat my pussy as well as you fucked it. Only then will I decide if I'm kicking you to the curb."

A slow grin spread across his face as he stood up with me in his arms and his dick still inside of me. How was this boy still hard? "I promise I won't disappoint you."

And he didn't. For the rest of the night and all through the next day, Walker Pierce showed me how he could please my body and make me come begging for more.

CHAPTER TEN

walker

EVERY NIGHT for the last two months of being inside of Pen had been like a dream. She tried to pretend like she wasn't in love with my cock, but she wasn't fooling me. When we were around the guys, she was as cool as a cucumber, but when we were alone, my sweet Pen burned hotter than the sun.

Much to her surprise, I wasn't tired of Pen. Not in the slightest, but I hadn't convinced her yet that she was the only woman I wanted to be buried deep inside. Every night, I left her sated in her bed, leaving only to sneak back inside the house I shared with the guys. Not that they noticed I was gone. They were too busy partying and fucking a new girl each night.

Now we were headed to the studio, where a tour bus was waiting for us. Everything was moving so fast; I could hardly believe we had recorded our first album. Tonight, we would be loaded up on the bus and driven to our first gig under Titan Records. One of the opening acts for Tragic Phenomenon had to drop out, and when we were asked if we'd like to take their place, we jumped at the chance. Never in my wildest dreams did I think I'd have the chance to open for one of my favorite bands.

We pulled into the parking lot of Titan Records, and parked out front was a huge black bus. All of our faces were glued to the windows as we took in what we hoped was our tour bus.

"Is that ours?" Kenton asked in awe, his jaw nearly to the floor.

"That is fucking sweet," Cross drew out the word. His leg bounced with excitement.

"I can't fucking believe it," Greer muttered from beside me. I looked at him from the corner of my eye, wanting to get a look at him. He had the faintest upturn of his lips as he tapped out a tune on the armrest. I couldn't remember the last time I saw even the semblance of a smile from him. Maybe he'd be better. Happier. I only wished I knew why he was an epic asshole most of the time. As if he could feel me staring, Greer glanced my way. I was surprised when he actually full-on smiled at me. "We fucking did it."

I clapped him on the back. "Hell, yeah, we did. All those years of hard work paid off."

The second the car stopped, we all piled out and ran to the bus. The door was open, and we pounded up the short set of stairs. We halted when we found Pen standing in a small kitchen area with a wide smile on her face. "What do you think, boys?"

"Is this ours?" I rushed out. If it wasn't, we were going to be sorely disappointed after seeing this beauty.

Pen spread her arms out to her side and twirled around in a circle. "It's all yours."

"Sick," Cross pushed by Pen and started inspecting every inch of our new home.

Everything was black, the furniture, the countertops, the tables. Even the wall of beds was black. There was a TV hung up on the wall with a couple of gaming systems underneath it. I wasn't much a gamer, but the rest of the guys were. It was smart to give them something to do during our downtime besides trash the place and drink.

"Pick your beds, and when you come back, we'll draw for who gets the bedroom in the back for a week." Pen pointed to the closed door at the end of the bus.

"Hey, there's already a bag on one of these beds," Kenton shouted as he patted the top bunk. "This one right here is mine." It wasn't surprising he wanted the top; Kenton was one tall motherfucker.

"Do we have another bandmate we don't know

about?" I asked as I eyed the bag on the bottom righthand bunk.

"That's mine." Pen's gaze flashed to mine before she looked away. Why hadn't she mentioned this before? "I won't always ride with you, especially during the day, but I was hoping you'd let me sleep here instead of the van."

Cross nodded his head as he took the middle bunk above hers. "Yeah, of course. We won't make you sleep in a van every night." He tapped his chin as he bit back a smirk. "What if we want to bring someone on board?"

"Well, they won't be spending the night unless you plan to drop them off at the next venue." Pen tapped her fingernail to her pink-painted lips. "Something you might need to think about."

"Fuck, that never crossed my mind. There's no way I'm bringing someone with me." Cross shook his head rapidly as if spending more than the time required to fuck someone was appalling to him. "Just make sure to give us time before we leave, so we can get our— "

I slapped him in the back of the head before he finished his sentence. "I think she gets it. You don't need to be so crude."

"What the fuck?" Cross rubbed the back of his head like I'd damaged him in some way.

"Suck it up. It wasn't that hard," I grumbled.

"Damn," Cross moaned, walking toward the front of the bus. "I'm going to go get my shit."

Pen trailed behind him. "You can put most of it underneath. There isn't room for much in the bunks."

Cross gave her a thumbs up and then glared my way. He flipped me off before he descended down the stairs.

"I guess we should go get our stuff," Kenton mumbled as he passed by.

Once everyone else was off the bus, Pen turned to me with turbulent golden eyes. "You didn't need to do that. I'm a grown woman and know what happens on and off the bus. I don't expect them or you to be celibate on this tour. In fact, I encourage it."

I cocked my head to the side. "You encourage it. Really? Are you saying you won't care if I'm with someone else? I think that's a lie, my sweet Penny."

"I'm not saying that." She leaned back against the kitchen counter and crossed one leg over the other. "What I'm saying is it will be better for *everyone* if they don't have any pent-up sexual frustrations."

I stalked the few feet that separated us. My mouth brushed against her pretty pink lips as I said. "Does that mean you're going to be fucking me on the regular?"

"I shouldn't," she shook her head and looked toward the front. "If we keep this up, we're apt to get caught."

"And you can't risk that," I finished for her. I'd heard it

time and time again. "Do you think the guys are going to say something to get you fired if they find out?"

"I don't know," she shrugged. "Maybe. You can't tell me Greer wouldn't love the chance to fuck with my life."

No, I couldn't. He was even more aggressive with her, although I wasn't sure why. Everything with him was a big-ass question mark.

"We'll find a way," I assured her.

"But maybe we should lay off." Pen turned around and started to place the water bottles that were on the counter into the small fridge. "I don't want to hold you back."

I pushed up against her and let her feel how hard I was for her. Whenever Pen was in a hundred-foot radius, my dick knew it and was begging to be inside of her. "The only person you're holding back is yourself, but if that's how you want to play it, then so be it."

"I think it's what's best for the both of us. I can keep my job, and you can do what you want without worrying about me." She nodded her head and sniffed.

Turning Pen around, I took in her glassy eyes. "Why are you doing this if this isn't what you want?"

"I…" Pen was cut short when the guys bounded up the stairs. Cross threw one of my bags at me, hitting me square in the chest, and then continued to walk by.

"We put the rest of your stuff underneath, dick smack," Greer growled as he fell onto one of the couches.

"Who's up for a…" he leaned forward and examined the games that were neatly lined up by the PlayStation. "Tournament of Call of Duty?"

"Oh, you're on, asshole. I'm going to kick all of your asses," Kenton laughed. He looked to Pen. "Are you in?"

She gave him a sad smile and sniffed. "Not today. I'm going to ride in the van, so you guys can enjoy your bus without me."

Kenton looked up at her with his sad puppy dog eyes, not understanding why Pen didn't want to hang out with us. "But you're going to sleep here, right?"

"Yeah, later tonight, when we stop for dinner, I'll get on. You boys have fun, but don't break anything. We've got a long tour."

The guys saluted her and then went back to fighting over who was going to play first.

"Before I go, let's see who gets the bedroom first?" Pen pulled a hat out of a bag that had been sitting on one of the tables. It already had tiny pieces of paper in it, but I wasn't paying attention to the hat. I was looking at the logo on the hat. It had our album name, Twisted Youth, on it, and in big letters, it said Crimson Heat. I couldn't take my eyes off it. We had come so far; I knew our lives would be irrevocably different by the time we were done touring. I only hoped it didn't change us for the worse.

"Do you like it?" She asked softly.

"What's not to like? I want one of my own." I tipped my head to the hat, and all the guys agreed. Each of us stared at it with wide excited eyes—even Greer.

"Oh, you're all getting a whole wardrobe, don't worry. I'll give it to you tonight."

I nodded my head, dumbfounded at the sight. I had a feeling that for the next few days, I was going to continue feeling out of my element as our dreams came true.

"Who would like to do the honors of pulling out the name?" Pen asked.

Without a word, Cross stuck his hand in the hat, pulled out a piece of paper, and read it. "Pen." He narrowed his eyes at her. "Is this rigged?"

"Nope, I guess I'm just lucky." Her eyes met mine with the saddest smile on her face. "Keep pulling them out. That's the order we'll go in."

Cross continued pulling out names until I was the last one pulled out. Maybe it was a good thing Pen had ended things. I wasn't sure how we'd get away with sleeping together inside those tiny bunks. Still, I had four weeks to figure out how to get her back into bed with me before I took up residence in the bedroom.

CHAPTER ELEVEN

pen

WHAT HAD I DONE? It had only been a few days that I'd been away from the band, and I was miserable. Well, not when I was with Stella, but I was as I laid here on the uncomfortable twin-size bed alone in my room while Stella was most likely getting some from the hottie crew member. Not that I blamed her. She deserved it after her ex made their divorce as difficult as possible. Plus, Remy was hot and if I wasn't hung up on a certain lead singer, I would have been salivating for him.

I tried to convince myself that calling off whatever it was that I had with Walker was the right thing to do, but I missed him so damn much. I shouldn't have slept with him in the first place, but I thought it was going to be a one-and-done kind of thing. Instead, I became addicted to the orgasms he gave me and how sweet he was to me.

Picking up my phone from the bedside table, I opened Instagram wanting to see Walker's face and see how last night's show had gone without me there. Typing in the hashtag, Crimson Heat, I instantly regretted my decision. There were multiple pictures of Walker with scantily clad girls pushing their big breasts into his side, against his arm, and he was… happy. Or at least he looked happy. Walker rarely smiled in public. He was the epitome of the bad boy rocker to his fans.

"Hey, why the sad face?" Stella asked, scaring me nearly half to death.

Pressing my hand over my rapidly beating heart, I took in a stuttered breath. "Oh, my God, Stella, knock or something."

"In the room we're sharing?" she eyed me skeptically, and then her eyes went wide. "Oh, did I interrupt something? Were you looking for porn?"

I rolled my eyes at her. "I can go without masturbating for the duration of the trip, and if I couldn't, I'd do it in the shower or something."

"Then what is it?" Stella sat down next to me on my tiny bed and looked in the direction of my phone that was lying face down on the bed.

"I was checking in on the boys," I admitted sheepishly. I had promised no work, and while it wasn't working, I hadn't told Stella about Walker and me. Something I was so thankful for now that we weren't… together. Anything to each other? I didn't know what we once were.

Stella narrowed her eyes at me. "I thought we said there would be no working while we're on vacation."

"I know, but I didn't want to go hang out with the rest of the ladies, so I thought I'd check online." I chewed on the inside of my cheek, waiting for her to admonish me.

Lying back, Stella rested her head on my stomach. She turned to look at me. "Are they being good little boys while you're away?"

"As far as I can tell. I didn't look much, and I didn't call to check-in or anything like that." Lifting a strand of her black hair, I twisted it around my finger. "Let's not talk about my work. Tell me how it went with Remy."

Her cheeks pinked as she looked up at the ceiling. "The man knows how to please a woman. I can say that."

"That's my girl. I'm glad you got a good dicking."

"Oh, my God, Pen. I can't even with you," she laughed.

"Are you going to hook up with him again?" Since I wasn't having sex, maybe I could live vicariously through my best friend.

"I want to. There's no doubt about that, but it's not so easy here on the boat. Those women are always swarming. Especially Ophelia."

"Oh, yeah, she wants him bad and hates the fact that

he can't hide how much he wants you instead of her. I'm assuming since you had sex with him that you talked to him about Ophelia saying he was with her last night."

"I did," she nodded. "He admitted to sleeping with her on the first boat he worked on."

"Oh, do you think you're going to become obsessed with him like she is?" I joked.

"Oh, fuck you," she giggled and pushed on my leg. "I will not become obsessed. After we leave Spain, I'll never see him again."

"Are you saying you're not going to rent us a yacht every year when you become a famous author?"

She rolled her head back and forth on me. "As nice as this is, besides Reagan being a raging bitch, I'll never spend this much money on a vacation. I don't care how much money I make." She smiled sleepily. She was probably dick drunk. "What about you?"

"I'll never be rich or famous, so... no private yachts for me."

Stella yawned. "I'm tired. I think I'm going to take a quick shower and go to sleep."

"Are you okay?" I asked her as she stood up and walked slowly to our bathroom.

Stella turned at the doorway and looked back at me. "Yeah, why wouldn't I be? I just had the best sex of my life."

"I don't know, but if you need me, I'm here. Always."

Her face softened. "I know, and the same goes for you. I worry about you being on the road all the time with a bunch of stinky boys."

She wasn't wrong about them being stinky, but they were also becoming something like family. I liked how they were a unit, and even though Greer was an ass ninety-nine percent of the time, they still included him in everything they did.

"Don't worry about me. I can handle those boys. They're harmless." Or at least I thought they were. Seeing those pictures of Walker was like a dagger to my heart. I guess I should have been happy it happened now and not when I got attached to him.

Or at least that's what I was telling myself. If I didn't have any feelings for him, I wouldn't be upset about those women snuggled up to him.

CHAPTER TWELVE

walker

THE MOMENT I saw Pen standing backstage, I wanted to walk off and take her in my arms even though I knew I couldn't. She'd been gone a week, and it had felt like an entire year went by in her absence. I wasn't any closer to convincing her we were good together than the day we started our tour, and she ended things. That's not how I thought things were going. I had planned to have her in my bed night after night. The thought of her being only a few feet away was soothing, even if we couldn't sleep next to each other. What I wouldn't give to have her sleep beside me for one night. Now, I wasn't sure if I'd ever get her back to get the chance.

Finishing our final song of the night, I looked out to the crowd and was still amazed this was my life. There were thousands of people out there every night we played, listening to our music and singing along to some of our songs.

I watched as, one by one, the guys left the stage and hugged Pen as they went by her. Okay, not Greer, but he didn't hug anyone. Ever. I followed suit and pulled her into my arms when I came up to her. I breathed in her citrus scent and never wanted to let go. Pen had other ideas. She patted me on the back and pulled back immediately.

I walked alongside her to the green room, keeping as much space between the rest of the band and us as possible. Leaning down, I spoke quietly enough that no one else would hear. "I missed you. Did you have fun on your vacation?"

When Pen told us she was leaving us for a week to go on vacation, I wasn't happy. At the time, I thought she was doing it to get away from me and put some space between us. Then I thought for sure she was going to use that time to get us a new manager.

I'd been wrong. I could admit that.

Her head whipped my way, and her whiskey eyes narrowed into slits as she looked at me. "I'm sure you weren't lonely for long."

Grabbing her bicep, I stopped us in the middle of the hallway. "What are you talking about?"

Pen pulled her arm from my hold and started walking. "Don't act like you don't know. Don't mistake me for convenience. You can get a different girl each night to sate your needs."

What?

Before I could even open my mouth, Pen opened the door to the green room. She went around to each guy and asked them how they were doing and if they needed anything. Well, almost all. Pen didn't even look my way before she was on her phone and ordering something for Kenton. Once Pen was done, she put her phone in the back pocket of her jeans. She looked up at us and smiled.

"Did you miss me?" She asked with a look that said she knew we had.

"Are you fucking kidding us? Cristiano is the biggest asshole. We didn't know how good we had it until you were gone." Kenton went down on his knees with his hands up like he was praying. "Please don't ever leave us again. You don't have any other vacations planned, do you?"

Stepping forward, she ruffled his shaggy hair. I nearly growled at seeing her touch another guy even when I knew it was only friendly. "Not that I know of. It was for my best friend." Her lips turned down as she thought of Stella. "She really needed the getaway, and who can say no to a private yacht."

Cross stepped to her with wide eyes. I was shocked he was so in awe of her vacation. "You were on a private yacht? No wonder you didn't check in on us."

"Well, the reception wasn't great where we were, and the Wi-Fi was spotty at best. I did check your social media once to see how you were all fairing." Her eyes slid to me. "And Cristiano sent me a report every night you had a gig."

"Was the yacht ballin'?" Cross pulled Pen across the room to the couch. "Do you have any pictures?"

"Of course, I have pictures. Do you really think I'd go on a private yacht and not take pictures?" She giggled. Fucking giggled. "But I'm not sure you want to see a bunch of women in their thirties in bikinis," she laughed, shaking her head.

I sure as fuck wanted to see her in a bikini, but I didn't want anyone else to see what she looked like, barely covered by some flimsy material.

Cross tipped his head toward her, looking Pen in the eyes. "If they look anything like you, I want to see. But…" he drew the word out like he didn't care if he saw or not. I knew he did since he was paying so much attention to the subject. "If you want to skip the pictures you're in, that's cool."

"Where'd you go?" Kenton asked, sitting beside her.

There was no way Penelope was going to get out of showing the pictures with both of them on her like flies on shit.

"Spain," she sighed out. "It was beautiful, and I think my Stella got her groove back while we were there."

Kenton lifted a brow. "And did our dear, sweet manager get her groove back as well?"

Pen looked up. Her gaze locked with mine. "No, but mine wasn't lost to begin with. If you really want to see some pictures, I'll show you, but if you want to greet any of the ladies from tonight, I can show you later."

"Fuck them. We've missed you. Let's get out of here and get some dinner. You can show us while we cram a bunch of carbs in our system."

Pen stood, pulling out her phone and tapping on it for a second. She was probably letting the bus driver know we would be coming out soon and to be ready. "I like the sound of that." She patted her stomach through her Crimson Heat band tee. "I think I gained at least ten pounds with all the amazing food the chef made for us, but I can never turn down carbs."

"Oh, Penny," Kenton wrapped an arm around her shoulders. "If you gained ten pounds, it went to all the right places. You look damn fine to me. In fact, I'd say you look radiant."

"Oh, that's just my Spain tan." She swatted at him, and I nearly lost my mind. What in the living hell was going on? Kenton didn't flirt with Pen. None of them did. Why were they all up in her business and touching her like they had a right to? The urge to kick their asses was bubbling to the surface.

"Whatever it is, you look damn fine," Cross said, pulling her away from Kenton and toward the door.

I pushed them both off her and turned on them. If it was possible, I would have shot laser beams out of my eyes at them and turned them to dust. "Give the woman some space."

"Oh, they're fine. I think it's sweet they missed me." She sashayed down the hall like she was on a runway. While I always thought Pen was sexy, there was definitely something different about her. Did she meet someone while she was away?

I hurried to her side and fought the need to touch her. I wanted to take her hand in mine, wrap my arm around her waist and pull her into me. Instead, I had to make do with being near her as I walked. "And you don't think it's sweet I missed you?"

She kept walking and didn't even bother to look in my direction as she spoke. "I think you mean you missed me more than they did, but maybe I'm wrong. Maybe you mean it the exact same way as they do, and if that's the case, then yes, I do believe you missed me because you had to deal with an insufferable Cristiano."

Even though I heard the guys hot on our heels, I moved in front of Pen, forcing her to stop and look at me. I waited until they passed to speak. "You know, I meant it as more, and I did fucking miss you. Why are you saying that? I wouldn't lie to you."

"I don't want you to have to lie to me either." She looked down and shook her head. "Just forget everything I said. It doesn't matter anyway."

"Of course, it fucking matters. I thought I was going crazy when you ended things, but when you were gone, I thought what you told us was some made-up story, and you were looking for someone else to manage us."

Her head shot up, and she glared at me. "I wouldn't do that, and for you to think that proves that I was right to end things." Pen moved around me and was out the door before I could stop her again.

Looking up to the ceiling like it could give me answers, I shouted. "How?" Only there was no one there to give me any answers. Hanging my head, I trudged my way out the door and onto the bus. I didn't bother to look at anyone as I pushed past them and slid into my bunk. Grabbing my headphones from beside the wall, I turned on my music and blasted it, so I wouldn't have to hear them laughing and talking about her trip. I would go ballistic if I heard any one of them say something about how hot she looked in her bikini.

For the sake of the band, I kept to myself for most of the night. I didn't come out when they went into the restaurant to eat. It wasn't until late at night, and I could feel we'd traveled at least a couple of hundred miles, that I used the bathroom and went in search of some food in our tiny kitchen. There wasn't much. Some popcorn that Kenton loved and a box of Pop-Tarts Cross ate. I hadn't stocked anything for me since I didn't think I'd be a needy bitch when Pen got back.

A slight noise from behind me had me turning around to find Pen sitting on one of the couches that took up the right side of the bus. She was curled up with a blanket over her legs, and there was something in her hands.

I cleared my throat, and when she didn't look up from what she was doing since she was most likely ignoring me, I asked. "What are you doing out here?"

Without looking up from what she was doing, she spoke quietly. Something I should have been doing if I cared about waking up the other people traveling on the bus with us, but I didn't. The only thing I cared about right then was Pen and why she'd been acting the way she had toward me.

"If you must know what I'm doing, I'm reading." She set down what looked like some type of device. "I'm reading my friend Stella's book."

"I know who Stella is." I stepped toward her. "Why are you acting like you don't know me?"

She stood, throwing the blanket that fell to the floor

back onto the couch. "I'm not acting like anything. I do know you. Now, if you don't mind, I'm going to sleep." Pen stormed off, slipping into her bunk.

Why did her words sound like an accusation?

Pen had only been back a few hours, and already I couldn't take the hostility toward me that was radiating off her. I had to know what was going on. Before she left, Pen did everything she could to not be alone with me, but this was a whole other level.

Pulling back the curtain to her bunk that was way too close to the ground for my height, I pushed Pen over as I laid down beside her.

"What are you doing?" She hissed.

"Since you seem so hell-bent on leaving any time I'm around, I decided to take matters into my own hands." I turned on my side, blocking her in.

"I could get out if I wanted," she whisper-yelled.

Bring my mouth to her ear, I whispered back. "You could, but you'd wake everyone up, and I know you don't want to do that."

"You're an asshole." She placed her hands on my chest and pushed. I was sure she meant to move me, but it did nothing but infuriate me further.

"I never said I wasn't. Now tell me why you're mad at me." My lips brushed the shell of her ear as I tried to be quiet and not wake up the rest of the bus.

"Just let me go to sleep," she huffed, trying to turn away from me, but I had her pinned up against the wall of the bus. Damn, maybe these tiny ass bunks were good for something.

"I'll leave you alone if you tell me why you're mad." But would I really? Doubtful. I was never going to leave her alone until she relented herself to me, body, mind, and soul.

The only sound for several long moments was our breathing. I could wait all night if I had to. Just being this close to her soothed the savage beast inside of me that broke out once she ended us.

"Fine, but once I tell you, I want you out of my bunk." Pulling away enough for our gazes to lock, she raised one lone eyebrow. "Deal?"

"Deal." I'd say anything in that moment to get her to talk to me and to find out what the hell happened while she was away. Was she pregnant with my baby? My hand instinctively went to her stomach.

"Don't touch me, either," she growled like a tiny kitten.

Putting my hands at my sides, I waited. "Fine, just tell me what's got you acting like this."

"Do you know what I saw the one and only time I looked you guys up on social media?"

"Not really. You know I don't go on there." Social media was not my thing. It was all negative assholes who thought they could do better or women wanting to have our babies. The extremes were too much for me to handle.

"Well, I'll tell you since you wanted to know so damn much. All I saw were picture after picture of women draping their bodies all over you. Which I get because you have to take pictures, but I saw the look on your face, and you were enjoying it a whole hell of a lot. So, there you go. You don't need me; you've got a gaggle of women lined up at your door to service you. Now, if you don't mind, I'd like to go to sleep." Pen pushed on me again, and this time I let her.

Pen wasn't mad. No, she was jealous, and jealousy was something I could work with. Now, I just had to figure out the best way to use that to my advantage.

CHAPTER THIRTEEN

pen

FROM THE CORNER of my eye, I saw Kenton nudge Cross as they played some video game. I was trying to read what Stella had sent to me of her book, but I was having a hard time concentrating. Ever since Walker joined me in my bunk last night, I couldn't get him out of my head. "What's got him in such a chipper mood?"

"Fuck if I know. He was one moody ass bitch while Pen was away, and now it's like he's walking on sunshine. I kind of want to stab him," Cross answered.

I looked up from my Kindle and was met with their smiling faces. "No stabbing anyone. Even band members," I said before I went back to my attempt at reading.

"Do you know why Walker's in such a pleasant mood?" Kenton leaned forward, waiting for my reply.

"No, I idea. Maybe one of your groupies made his night. I don't know. That's not really part of my job."

"I heard you two fighting last night," Cross muttered.

"Good for you," I rolled my eyes at him when what I really wanted to do was snap at him for listening. "If you heard, then you should know your guess is as good as mine on why he's in such a good mood."

Cross held his hands up and scooted back on his side of the bus. "I had my headphones in, so I couldn't make out what you were saying. I only heard you two arguing."

"If you're so interested in why Walker's acting the way he is, then why don't you ask him?"

Kenton's face scrunched up as he looked down the hall at the bunks. "It's not his week to get the bedroom, is it?"

"No, fucker, it's my turn. Don't act like you didn't know," Cross hit some buttons on his controller and then growled. "You cheated."

"How did I cheat?" Kenton threw out there.

Fighting over games was typical on the bus. It kind of made me wish I hadn't got them a PlayStation to begin with. I guess it was better than them watching porn. Listening to a bunch of moans from the living area would have been pretty awkward. Why hadn't I packed my noise-canceling headphones? Maybe I needed to order a new pair and have them delivered to a future venue. Then I wouldn't have to listen to their chatter.

Cross set down his controller and moved into the kitchen. "Does anyone need a drink?"

"I'm good, thanks."

"Hey, Walk," Cross moved to stand beside Walker as he folded some clothes and put them into a bag.

"What's up?" Walker asked without stopping what he was doing.

Cross bumped his shoulder into Walker's and looked back over his shoulder. I looked down quickly, hoping he didn't see me looking at them over my Kindle. "Do you have any more of whatever you're on?"

"Fuck off," Walker growled. "You know I don't do drugs. I don't even take ibuprofen, asshole."

"Seriously though, what's up with you? Why are you so happy?" Cross leaned back against the wall of other bunks.

Walker lifted one shoulder. "Why wouldn't I be in a good mood? We're living the dream."

"That we are." He paused for a long moment. "Does your mood have anything to do with Pen being back?"

I kept my focus on the same sentence I'd been reading for at least the last thirty minutes and pretended like I wasn't listening to every word they spoke.

"Sure, I'm happy she's back. Aren't we all? But she's not the reason why I'm in a good mood."

"Well, are you going to share with the class why?" Kenton yelled from across from me.

"No real reason. Does there have to be a reason why I'm in a good mood?"

"Not all, but you're not usually… chipper."

"I have a good feeling about tonight's show. Plus, we get to sleep in real beds tonight. Aren't you happy to spend a night off the bus?"

"Fuck man, I can't wait to take a long shower and not get bitched out about using all the hot water," Kenton moaned as if imagining already being in the shower.

"Fuck a shower. I'm going to take a nice hot bubble bath. Preferably with at least a couple of women in it." A wicked grin spread across Cross's face.

"Yo, who said the tub was going to be big enough for one of us, let alone with multiple people?" Greer asked, annoyed. Or at least it sounded more annoyed than usual. It was difficult with him. I gave up on being friends with Greer.

I could feel all their eyes turned to me.

Kenton slid in beside me and tugged me to his side. "Pen, do you know what type of rooms we're getting?"

I grinned and pushed myself away. "I do, but I'm not going to tell you. You'll just have to wait and see."

Cross moved in front of me and got down on his knees. "At least give me an idea how many girls I should bring back to my room."

"Oh, my God, I want no part in your orgy. I don't

remember looking at the bathtubs, but just to be safe, why don't you only bring back one girl." I paused, wondering if I should say what I was going to say next, but decided I would. It was my job to look out for them. "Don't have any girls spend the night. I know how that sounds, but you don't want them to feel special and get attached unless you're feeling the same."

"Oh," Cross jumped up and backed up until he fell back onto the couch directly across from me. "Trust me; I'm not looking for anything long-term. That screams disaster from a mile away." He took in a shuddering breath. "What if I need help kicking a girl out? Can I come to you to get them ushered away safely?"

"Don't be a fool," Walker growled out. "Pen isn't here to get you laid or to help you kick girls out of your bed. If you're going to stick your dick into anyone, you should have the balls to tell them to leave."

My thoughts exactly, but I wasn't going to express that with Walker in the room. I was even more annoyed with his happy mood. Did he enjoy knowing I saw him with those other girls, and it bothered me? If that was the case, then he could go fuck himself. I wasn't going to be helping any of them get their dicks wet.

"Ah, really? What if she's a stage five clinger?"

Setting down my Kindle, I blew out an irritated breath through my nose. "If you're so worried about it, then you need to do better at picking women. But if you need help, I'll kick their ass to the curb. It will be a one-time thing, and then there will be no more girls for any of you."

Let's see how they liked that prospect.

"If you need help, come get me. I'll happily end whoever's night of fun," Greer joined in.

"Well, thanks for that, mate," Cross said in a horrible Australian accent.

"Just don't be stupid. I know you're all young and like having fun, but make sure you're wrapping it up. You don't want to end your career because you got a disease from some groupie." I hated what I was about to say, but it needed to be said. "I'll stop by the pharmacy and make sure your rooms are stocked with condoms. When you run out, let me know, and I'll get you more. Deal?"

"Deal," Kenton, Cross said in unison. It didn't go unnoticed that Walker didn't agree, but the guys didn't seem to care. They were too busy dreaming up fantasy girls to fuck that night and the nights to come.

CHAPTER FOURTEEN

pen

AFTER GIVING myself an orgasm with the showerhead in my hotel bathroom that was nowhere near as fulfilling as the ones Walker gave, I landed on the bed and snuggled into the thick down comforter, and promptly fell asleep with Walker taking up every square inch of the space in my head.

I dreamt of him, and they were good dreams too. Dreams of him using his hands and tongue on me to bring me to release. Not of him having sex with every girl he came into contact with, which would have helped me get over him that much faster.

My phone rang, waking me up. For a second, I didn't remember where I was. I'd been in Spain only days ago, then on the bus, and now the hotel. I patted around on the bed for my phone, and when I finally found it underneath my pillow, I checked the time to see it was three in the morning, and Walker was calling me. If he was calling to get some girl out of his room, I was going to strangle him to death.

"What is it, Walker?" It came out harsher than intended, but I wasn't happy about being woken up in the middle of the night on one of our few nights in a hotel.

"Shit," he croaked out, sounding dreadful. "I'm…" he coughed and then spoke again, his voice cracking. "I'm sorry for waking you up, Pen, but I feel awful. I can't get room service on the phone, and I can't figure out how to make a cup of hot water with this damn coffee pot. Can you come to my room?"

My heart softened at hearing him speak and sounding so pitiful. "What are your symptoms? Surely there's an all-night place where I can pick you up something?"

"I don't need any medicine," he sniffed. "A hot cup of tea or lemon water is all I need."

I wasn't so sure about that, but I remembered overhearing him talking to Cross earlier in the day, and he mentioned rarely taking any medications.

"I'll come see if I can figure it out." Maybe all he really needed was a hot cup of tea, but from the cracking in his voice and the way he sounded stuffed up, I wouldn't bet on it.

"Thanks, Pen. That would be great. I'll leave the door cracked, so you can get in. I need to lie down."

Before I could tell him it wasn't a good idea to leave his door open, Walker hung up.

Hopping out of bed, I threw on a pair of sweatpants, a tank top, and a hoodie before I was out the door and on my way down the hall to Walker's room. There were a few noises coming from Cross and Kenton's rooms that I tried my best to ignore. What they did was their own business as long as there weren't any girls causing problems afterward.

I knocked on Walker's door before I stepped inside. I didn't think he had anyone in his room, but if he did, I hoped they were dressed.

"Come in," he croaked out.

"You really shouldn't leave your door open, nor should you tell anyone to just come into your room. You know that, right?" I said as I rounded the corner to where his bed sat.

Walker let out a tired breath. He had dark circles under his eyes, and he was a sickly shade of white instead of his usual olive skin tone. He looked as bad as he sounded on the phone.

Without thought, I moved across the room and sat beside him on the bed. The second my hand touched his forehead, he let out a soft sigh. Walker was burning up.

"I don't think a cup of tea is going to fix you. You're

sick. Really sick. You need to take something to bring the fever down. I can run to the pharmacy and get you some NyQuil. It will help you sleep too."

He shook his head as he pulled the covers up under his chill. "I don't want to take all that shit. It's not good for you."

"What's not good for you is having a high fever. You have to at least take something to bring it down. It's why you have the chills."

He looked up at me with sad eyes. "Can I just start with the tea and see how it goes?"

"Fine," I gave in, hoping that once he drank his tea Walker would realize how it wasn't the cure for what ailed him.

I went over to the other side of the room and stared down at the coffee pot. For a moment, I was too tired to figure out how to even turn it on. I swore hotels liked to make these things impossible to use in order for you to call room service or use the coffee shop they had in the lobby.

I kept my back to Walker, not wanting to look at him being all pitiful. It felt like forever as I waited for the water to heat up and pour into the tiny cup. I steeped the tea bag into the hot liquid as I walked back over to the bed.

"I'm sorry they don't have honey." I was sure most hotels didn't expect their guests to be sick while staying.

Walker was a singer and liked to have tea with honey in it, so from now on, I'd keep honey on me just in case.

"This will be fine. Thanks." He took the cup from me and blew on the hot tea before he took a sip.

"I don't know how you do it. I have to have sugar in my tea, or it just tastes... dry," I shuddered to even think about drinking non-sweet tea.

One corner of his mouth tipped up before he continued to drink more of his disgusting tea.

"If that is all, I'll go back to my room now." I looked down to see I'd forgotten shoes in my haste. I was lucky I'd gotten fully dressed with how quickly I'd left my room. What did that say about me?

"Can you stay with me for a little bit? I promise I won't try to hit on your or anything like that." He looked up at me with his big, black eyes that pleaded with me to stay.

Personally, I liked to be left alone when I was sick, but I knew some people didn't. I understood there was no one else that could come sit by his side while he was sick. It made me wonder about his family. If he wanted me to stay, then I was going to ask questions.

"Sure," I sat down on the bed and crossed my legs Indian-style, getting as comfortable as I could with Walker only being a foot away. "If you were home right now, who would be taking care of you?"

Walker lowered his tea and looked at me for a long moment. "I probably would have called you."

"That's not what I asked. If you didn't know me and I wasn't your manager, who would be by your side?"

"I don't know," he lazily shrugged as if it took all of his energy to make that one move. "Probably Kenton, but I wouldn't ask."

"What about your parents? Surely your mom would want to take care of you." I knew my mom would have if she were alive. I didn't talk to my dad. He was too controlling and didn't approve of the career I wanted. My brother, on the other hand, would drop everything to come to me if I called. So would Stella.

Walker laid down, moved to his side, and pulled the covers up until they reached his chin. He closed his eyes, and I thought he was going to go to sleep without answering me. I watched him, waiting for him to fall asleep so I could leave. There was still a chance I could get a decent night's sleep if I got back to my bed soon.

"My parents didn't think it was smart of me to drop out of college to chase a fool's dream." His eyes opened and locked on me. "Those are their words, not mine."

"I'm sorry," I frowned at him. "If it makes you feel any better, my dad feels the same way." I rubbed my hand along the blanket on his outstretched leg.

"How long has it been since you talked to him?" he asked quietly.

I kind of stepped in that, didn't I?

"My dad is a hard ass, and he's not one to gauge parents on." I tried to backtrack, but even sick, I knew Walker wasn't buying it.

"How long, Pen?"

"Ten years." It was shocking to hear those words. It sounded so long, and yet I wouldn't change my decision. "My brother and I are incredibly close, though. Unfortunately, he lives in South Carolina, and I hardly see him. He's got two young boys, and that makes traveling difficult."

"It's nice that you have him. I'm an only child, or at least I think so." He closed his eyes and shuttered.

"What do you mean you think so?" How could he not know?

Walker huffed out a breath and tightened his eyes as if it would keep the bad away. "Because my dad is a serial cheater, and I wouldn't be surprised if he got multiple women pregnant."

That had to be difficult to know about your dad. People cheated. All the time, but to know one of your parents was cheating would be horrible.

"I promised myself I'd never be like him. I'll never cheat on you," he whispered. I wasn't sure if he was falling asleep or if his throat hurt. He didn't sound as stuffed up as he did on the phone, so maybe the tea did help somewhat.

"We're not together, but whoever you end up with will be one lucky lady." I stood and patted his leg. "Get some sleep, and hopefully, you'll feel better in the morning. If you need anything, you can call me."

One eye cracked open, following me as I made my way around his bed. "What if I need you here? Would you stay with me?"

"I don't think that's a good idea, Walker." I couldn't let my heart thaw just because he was sick and needy.

"Please," he begged. "You can sleep in here, and I promise to keep my hands to myself. I'll even turn the other direction, so I'm not breathing my germs on you."

"I think you'll be fine without me." I stood my ground, not giving in.

"I really won't. I think I got sick because you won't talk to me, and I've been wracking my brain trying to figure out how to get you back."

"You never had me, Walker. It was only sex. I'm convenient right now, but I promise you, you'll find someone else once you're not sick."

He sat up as if lightning struck him dead in the chest and reached over to grab me. He hauled me onto the bed and held me still as I tried to fight him. He was surprisingly strong for being sick. I also wasn't fighting him as hard as I could have. I liked the feel of his hands on me, even if it was for a reason other than sex. "What if I don't want anyone else?"

"Like I said, I'm convenient." I huffed, annoyed at myself for what I was about to say, but it needed to be said. "Didn't you like one of the women you were with when I was gone?"

He shook his head as his grip on me tightened. "I know the pictures you saw, but I can promise you, everyone kept their hands to themselves. I haven't been with anyone but you."

"And how am I supposed to believe that?" I started to fight harder to get out of his grasp, but Walker's hold on me only tightened.

"Because I've never lied to you. Did they offer to sleep with me? Yeah, they did. When I said no, one offered to blow me, and I said no to that as well. If you ask the guys, they'll confirm what happened when you were gone. Cristiano can confirm as well."

"Oh, right," I laughed bitterly. "You know I can't ask any of them because if I did, they'd know something was up between us, and I'd most definitely lose my job." Even though he was sick, I couldn't hide my irritation as I fell to my side with Walker's arms still around me and hissed out, "Or did you forget that?"

Walker let go of me. "Of course, I didn't forget. You're

all I think about, and I'm constantly trying to figure out a way for us to be together."

Not looking at him because I knew he'd see the truth on my face, I asked, "And what if I don't want to be with you?"

"We both know that's a lie." He turned on his side with his back to me. "I don't want to fight you while I'm miserable. Please, don't leave once I fall asleep."

"Why shouldn't I?"

He looked over his shoulder at me. "Because as much as you don't want to, you like me."

"I never said I didn't like you. I like all of you. Well, like might be too strong of a word for Greer, but I like the rest of you."

Walker fell onto his back and glared at me. "I don't like them flirting with you or you with them."

I couldn't help it; I started to laugh and couldn't stop. Clutching my stomach, I rolled onto my side and curled into a ball, trying to prevent peeing myself.

Walker growled, and the sound halted my giggles. "There's nothing funny about them flirting with you. I swear they're doing it to piss me off."

"Why isn't it possible they like me? I'm a fun girl."

"Oh, trust me, I know how fun you are, and it makes my blood boil to even think there's a possibility they want the same thing I do with you."

"You hush," I pushed him until he was on his side and facing away from me. "They don't want to be with me."

"They saw you in your bikini, and even though I didn't see it, I can only imagine how hot you looked in it. Now every time they look at you, they're imagining you naked."

Boys. They were so obsessed with sex. I didn't want to tell him they might be imagining me with my clothes off. It would set him off. The thing was. I didn't care how much they wanted to see me naked. It was never going to happen. I didn't see any of them the way I saw Walker.

Turning on my side, I pressed my back into Walker's and pulled the blanket up to cover us. "Stop being ridiculous, and get some sleep. And if you get me sick, it's going to be your ass taking care of me."

"I'd take care of you every day if you let me," he murmured into the quiet room before quickly falling asleep.

CHAPTER FIFTEEN

walker

WAKING UP, I felt like complete and utter shit. I was on fire. My skin was slick with sweat, and my mouth tasted like ass. I edged my feet out of the blanket, trying to cool down. It hurt to move even the smallest bit.

"Oh, thank God! I thought you were in a coma," Pen rushed out. Her hand ran up my arm and up to my forehead.

I rolled over to see her long caramel hair up in a messy bun. She was still in her sweatpants but now only had a tank top on that showcased her perfect tits. Looking up, I found her nibbling on her bottom lip. Gripping her hand in mine, I pulled it close to my chest. "I'm fine. Well, I'm not fine. I feel like death warmed over, but I think I'll live."

"Oh, you think you'll live, do you?" She laughed shakily. "I was this close to calling an ambulance." She held her hand up with her fingers apart only the tiniest amount. "Hopefully, it's just the flu, and you'll be fine in a couple of days. Otherwise, we'll have to cancel a show or two."

"No," I sat up with a groan. Pen's hands were on me, helping me sit up and covering my naked torso with the sheet. I held her hands to my chest. "You're not canceling anything. I'll be as good as new by our show in… wherever we'll be next. I just need to flush my body with a lot of liquids."

"Maybe you should think about taking some medicine." She placed the back of her delicate hand on my forehead. "You've still got a temperature."

"Having a temperature is a good thing. That means my body is fighting whatever it is I have."

"Yeah, until it gets too high, and you have a seizure or go into a coma," she said with big eyes and her tone as serious as a heart attack.

I scoffed and instantly regretted it. "How often do you think that happens?"

"I don't know, but it does happen. That's why they say you need to keep your temperature down." She pulled out her phone, and her face fell. "Shit, we need to be on the bus in thirty minutes. I'm going to text the guys and tell them you're taking the bedroom until you're better and it's disinfected."

I wasn't going to argue with her. The thought of being

jammed up in my bunk while my body ached and I felt like shit sounded like pure torture.

Needing to pack up my shit, I slid to the side of the bed. Looking back over my shoulder, I asked. "Can we get me some apple juice? Ice cold apple juice always makes my throat feel better."

Jumping up, Pen ran around to my side of the bed and pushed me down until I was flat on my back. "What are you doing?"

"Getting ready to leave. I have to pack what little I bought up last night," I explained as my body sagged into the bed. While I talked a big game, I wasn't sure how I was going to get on stage in a couple of days if I still felt this way.

"You just rest, and I'll pack up your things." Her phone started pinging with rapid-fire texts. With her attention diverted, I once again tried to haul my ass out of bed, but Pen must have had eyes in the back of her head because she pushed me down with a sweet little kitten growl. "Please don't make my life harder than it already is."

There was a pleading tone to her voice that had me giving in. "Fine, I'll let you do it all while I just lay here and watch you."

"Thank you." The exhale that came out of her was full of frustration. "The guys are fighting about me demanding the bedroom for you."

"Tell them I'll give up my week," I mumbled as I searched for my phone. I didn't like that they were putting even more stress on her. I found my phone the second she did. Pen grabbed it up and put it in my bag. "I can't even have my phone?" I whined. Even I sounded annoying to my own ears.

"No, you can't because I have a feeling you were going to engage with them, and I don't need you fighting my battles. If you're always stepping in, then they'll think I'm not capable."

She started to move, searching for more of my belongings, but I grabbed Pen's wrist and held it until she looked down at me. I can admit I didn't like feeling like an invalid, but I didn't mind Pen taking care of me. Maybe she'd soften up to me. At least she had last night, or else she wouldn't have stayed.

"We all know you are fully capable of kicking ass and taking names. This is just me trying to make your life easier in the short amount of time we have before getting on the bus. You still have to get your things as well."

"Fuck," she pulled away and moved around like a chicken with its head cut off. "I totally forgot about my stuff. Can you imagine if I had left it all here? What was I thinking?"

"You were thinking about me and taking care of me because you're a wonderful and selfless woman."

"Oh please," she rolled her eyes. "Don't kiss my ass. I am far from selfless. I'm doing my job."

"I don't believe anywhere in the contract states that you have to take care of us when we're sick." I followed her as she grabbed my hoodie and threw it on the bed. "If it was Cross or Kenton, would you have stayed?"

"Put that on," she pointed to my sweatshirt. She slung my bag over her shoulder and then grabbed my charger out of the wall. "In fact, I probably would have, but they wouldn't have asked."

No, they wouldn't have asked. I was the needy dickhead who couldn't get enough of her.

Pushing my arms through the sleeves of my hoodie, I took in how tired Pen looked. Had she even slept last night?

"Do you want to stay here while I get my things or— "

"I'll come," I interrupted her, wanting to be in her space. It felt like it had been years instead of a month since I'd been to her condo, breathing in everything that was Penelope Rose.

"Okay, we should hurry." She held open the door for me when it should have been the other way around.

"It's not like they're going to leave without us." I followed along like a lost kitten to her room and waited for Pen to open her door. She patted her sweatshirt and then her pants, a worried look etched on her face. This morning she looked more stressed than ever before. Pen was out of sorts, which was so unlike her.

She pulled the keycard out and grumbled as she walked inside. "I thought for a minute there that I ran out of here so fast that I forgot to grab my card. Well, I did, but I'm lucky I put it in my pants when I went to get ice last night."

I moved to sit on her bed. Happy to watch her from my perch as I took in her room. It was tidy, but that was to be expected. Pen kept everything nice and neat, and we'd only been here overnight. Staying at the hotel had been a treat. One that I was grateful for.

Outside the room, we heard loud voices pass by, and I knew it was Cross and Kenton joking around. Since we'd formed Crimson Heat, I'd wanted to be a part of that brotherhood, but as I sat here with Pen shuffling around getting her things together, I realized I'd much rather be in her space than theirs.

I wasn't sure when Pen had come to mean everything to me, but I was damn sure I was going to do everything in my power to make sure I became everything to her. I needed to show her there was no other woman for me, even when I had to smile at the cameras with women grabbing my ass and signing autographs on their overly inflated boobs. I might be young, but I knew what I wanted and what I wanted was my sweet Pen.

"Are you ready to go? I'm sure that was them that

sounded like a herd of cattle out there." A grin broke out on her face as she settled the two bags on her shoulder. "I'm not sure how three people can make so much noise."

I stood and tried to take my bag from Pen, but when her narrowed eyes fixed on me, I backed away and followed her out the door. "The sad thing is it was only Kenton and Cross. Greer was most likely staring ahead with a scowl on his face."

"Someday, you're going to have to tell me how you guys met. I can see why the rest of you are together, but not Greer. It's like he hates…"

"Everything," I supplied for her. "I'm not sure why but he does. He's never opened up to us. Maybe that's because Kenton and Cross have known each other for years." I hit the down arrow for the elevator, and it arrived in a matter of seconds. As we stepped inside, I continued. "They had a band, and when it split up, they wanted to continue to make music, so they held auditions. They found me first, and we bonded. I think Greer felt that and never tried to make friends. We both know neither one of us is going to replace Kenton or Cross, and we don't try. If Greer wasn't a kick-ass guitar player, we never would have asked him to join. Especially with his attitude, but we put up with it for the sake of the music." I shrugged as if it all made sense.

Pen nodded as we stepped off the elevator. We could see the bus sitting out front through the hotel's windows. "I can see that. But you guys are very welcoming, so it's his fault you're not better friends."

"I'm not sure how welcoming we really are," I chuckled lowly.

"You all welcomed me with open arms," she said as we stepped onto the bus.

"Yeah, and that had nothing to do with how beautiful you are or the fact that you believed in our music and wanted to get us a record deal," I said in my most sarcastic voice as I walked behind her.

"Oh, fuck, you do look bad." Kenton choked down a laugh as he stepped back to let me pass by. "I thought you'd faked being sick to get the bedroom, but now," he held his hands up and got as far away as he could. "I think you should take it. I don't want your nasty ass germs."

"Thanks," I grumbled as I trudged behind Pen. She opened the door to the bedroom and slipped inside.

"Don't come out until you feel better," Cross shouted.

I flipped him off even though I knew he couldn't see it. I would have yelled, but it would have only hurt my throat.

"I'm going to go talk to the driver and ask him to pull into a pharmacy, so I can get you that apple juice." Slumping down onto the bed, I glared up at her. You could get apple juice almost anywhere. We didn't need to go to a pharmacy. "Don't even start with me. It's better to have something in case you need it. We could be hours away from a store if you come to your senses."

"I'm not going to fight you. If it makes *you* feel better, then, by all means, buy out the pharmacy. Just because you buy it doesn't mean I'll take it, though."

Pen made an annoyed little noise in the back of her throat, and I could imagine her wanting to stomp her foot. "I'll be back once we hit the pharmacy."

Lying back on the bed, I closed my eyes. While I hated being sick, I didn't mind the extra attention from Pen since she'd been giving me the cold shoulder since she got back from her trip. Now I just had to figure out how to work it to my advantage.

CHAPTER SIXTEEN

pen

I COULD HEAR KENTON, Cross, and Greer clear across the store. They were running around like they'd never been inside of one before. If this was what it was like to have kids, then no, thank you. I'd gladly pass.

My thoughts immediately went to Walker, and I wondered if he wanted to have children someday.

I shook my hands out. It didn't matter because I wasn't with Walker, and I never would be. It didn't matter if he wanted kids or not. He wasn't my future.

It didn't really matter. I was getting too old to have children anyway. Thirty-seven was not the new twenty-five in relation to childbearing.

Stuffing my hand-held basket with everything known to man to help a cold and the flu, I made my way up to the front to check out. He may not want to take it, but if I got sick, I knew for damn sure I was going to take anything and everything to make me feel better. It wasn't like I could take a day off. Especially not after taking a trip during the middle of their US tour. I'd have to suck it up and go on like I wasn't sick.

The guys set down a wide range of items on the counter. They had jerky, beer, candy, chips, Lysol, and deodorant. I was thankful for the deodorant because things got stinky on the bus with four guys, and the driver and I were stuck in close proximity for long periods of time.

"Did you get everything you wanted?" They smiled like kids in a candy store and nodded their heads. Okay, Greer didn't, but he didn't look angry, so that was a plus. "Good because we're not making a habit out of this." I wasn't sure why I'd offered to buy them whatever they wanted except that I wanted them to keep quiet so Walker could rest.

Three hundred dollars later, I walked out of Walgreens with enough apple juice to choke a man. Kenton, Cross, and even Greer carried the bags onto the bus for me.

"Any other stops you need to make?" Charles asked.

"We're all set. I'm sorry to disrupt the schedule, but I think things will go much smoother now that we have supplies."

"Keep that boy back there. I don't want to get sick," Charles grumbled. He was usually sweet, but I understood. He couldn't drive for long hours if he was sick as a dog.

I put all the items away and the apple juice in the refrigerator before I headed to the back to check on Walker. Hopefully, he was sleeping and getting the rest he needed to get better. I wasn't sure how happy Titan Records would be if their opening act couldn't play. They'd have to find someone new for a show or two, and that would be a difficult task—one that would put me on Cristiano's bad side.

When I stepped through the bedroom door, I found Walker lying in bed, his eyes trained on the door. He'd taken his shirt off, and one bare foot hung out of the side of the blanket.

"Hey, how are you feeling? I put your juice in the fridge, but it will take a bit before it's cold. They didn't have any in the refrigerated section."

"Can you get me a bottle of water?" He sounded so tired, like he could fall asleep talking to me.

"Sure. Is there anything else I can get for you?" I asked as I started to walk out.

"Can you stay with me? I don't think I can call out loud enough for you to hear me if you're out there."

I didn't point out that he could call or text me. Maybe Walker was clingy when he was sick. I didn't know, but he looked so pitiful I couldn't deny him.

"We can watch anything you want." He pointed to the TV that was embedded in the wall. "Your pick."

Walker must have been desperate because he always complained about what I wanted to watch. Really, I didn't care what we watched most of the time. I didn't watch TV. I had other things to do with my time. I wasn't used to having free time to just chill out. The only time I made room for hanging out was with Stella. But I liked fighting with him about what to watch.

"Fine," I gave in. "I'll be back in a couple of minutes. You can pick what we watch but try to make it something I'll enjoy."

I'd barely slept all night. Walker's fevered body was always pressed against mine, making me feel like I was trying to sleep in a furnace. I'd probably last five minutes before I fell asleep as long as I kept some distance between us. And really, if that fucker got me sick, I was going to kill him. Well, first, I'd make him take care of me until I was healthy enough for me to kill him.

"Are you thinking murderous thoughts over there?" Kenton asked as I pulled out two water bottles.

"Possibly." I glanced over my shoulder. "Walker does that to me." I hesitated to ask, but my mouth was spitting out the words before I could catch myself. "Is he usually…" I couldn't think of a good word that wouldn't give away what had transpired between us.

"A big baby when he's sick," Cross supplied for me.

"Something like that. He wants me to watch TV with

him." I rolled my eyes. "So, I guess I'll be back there if you need me."

Cross moved across the tiny space in one stride. "We're grown men. While it's nice to have someone taking care of us after going so long without, we can get on without you."

"I know you can, but this is my job, and sometimes I feel like I'm doing a shit job."

Putting his hands on my shoulders, Cross leaned down until we were eye to eye. "You're doing a great job. You don't have to mother hen us to be doing your job. In fact, I don't think that's in the description of being a band manager."

"I don't know about that. Some bands need a lot of attention," I laughed.

"Yeah, well, we're not one of them. We're not out every night getting into trouble. The only thing we care about after our music is getting some pussy."

A surprised laugh burst out of me. Cross removed his hands from my shoulders only to drape one arm around me. "What? It's true, and we all know it."

"Yes, we do," I giggled. "And it's perfectly normal." I held up my phone. "If you need me, you can text me."

"But we won't," he said, breaking away to sit back down at the table. They had laid out everything they got from the pharmacy like a kid would lay out their candy from trick or treating on Halloween.

"Have fun with your goodies," I called over my shoulder as I stepped back into the bedroom. Closing the door, I turned to find Walker staring at me with a deep furrow between his brows.

"What was all that about?" He croaked out.

"Nothing," I waved him off as I moved toward the bed. I handed him his water bottle and sat at the end of the bed.

His voice was low, and what sounded like hurt echoed through his words. "Why are you all the way down there?"

"Because you're sick, and I don't want to get sick. Plus, this isn't some Netflix and chill session where we start off all curled up together. There's no more snuggling between us, remember?"

"Oh, I remember you calling it off. I still don't understand it, though."

"You don't need to understand it, Walker. What you need to do is respect my feelings and wishes."

"What about my feelings and what I want?" He asked so quietly that for a second, I thought I'd imagined the words.

"They are valid, the same as mine. We can agree to disagree on this. We can't be together and if you try, you'll move on and forget we ever had something between us."

"Is that what you did? Did you move on while you were

on vacation? Did you meet someone while you were in Spain?"

I turned around to face him fully, sitting with my knees to my chest and my arms wrapped around my legs. "I didn't meet anyone, nor have I moved on. I wish I had," I said more to myself than for him to hear.

Walker sat up, leaning back against the wall. "Why are you doing this to us? What can I do to prove to you that it's only you that I want?"

"You think I'm what you want. That is until you see some hot girl who wants to fuck you and then you have to turn her down. Then you'll start to resent me because I'm always around and you're stuck in a relationship with a woman who's old enough to be your mother." I pressed my forehead to my knees and tried to forget how he was begging me with his eyes to take him back.

Walker closed his eyes. His jaw was tight as he breathed in and out forcefully. "I'm never going to resent you. Well, I might but only because you're being so damn stubborn about giving us a real chance. I don't only want to fuck you. I want to share this whole amazing experience with you." I started to tell him he was, but he held his hand up. "Not like this. Not as my manager who's running things, but as my girlfriend who gets to see me grow. As the woman who I can serenade and who will cheer and sing along with the crowd."

Didn't he understand I already was most of those things? I wasn't his girlfriend, but I sang along with his songs and cheered for him on the sidelines.

"I can never be the woman out in the crowd for you, Walker. Not unless I'm not your manager. Is that what you want?" I asked, lifting up my head to look at him.

"That's not what I want. Not at all. I know how much you love your job, and I don't want to do anything that will take it away from you, but surely there's a compromise. Some way for us to be together while you're still our manager."

Resting my cheek to my knees, I closed my eyes. "I don't see a way. I didn't see it before, and I most definitely don't see it now. We'd have to keep our relationship hidden. Not just for a short period of time, but forever. Do you want to be my dirty little secret?"

"I'll be your anything. Whatever you can give me, I'll take."

"You say that now," I shook my head. "But the fun of having a secret will wear off, and then what? I don't want to fall any deeper than I already am because I know I'll shatter when this all comes to an end."

"I won't let you down, and if you fall, I fall. Hell, I've already fallen for you. I don't know when. Maybe it was the moment I saw you, or maybe it was one day at practice. I don't know," he shook his head, his charcoal eyes pleading with me to listen to him. "What I do know is you're in here," he pounded on his chest above his heart. "And I know you're never going to leave no matter how hard you try to push me away. So please, please stop pushing because I'm not going anywhere."

Tears streamed down my cheeks and rapidly fell as I listened to the most beautiful and heartbreaking words ever spoken to me. How could I deny Walker? How could I break both of our hearts?

I crawled up the bed and wrapped my arms around his neck as I buried my face into the crook of his shoulder. Walker wasted no time enveloping me into his warm, strong arms. "It's going to be okay. I've got you," he whispered onto the top of my head. He ran his hand down my hair and back and up again.

Pulling back enough for him to see how serious I was, I stared into his dark eyes filled with so much love it took my breath away. "Don't make me regret this."

"Never," he vowed. "Fuck, I wish I wasn't sick right now, so I could kiss you. I miss those pillowy soft lips of yours against mine."

"I missed you too." I ran my hand through the long strands of his hair. "You should rest though."

He nodded, his body slumping against the wall. "Will you snuggle with me? I can hold you from behind and maybe you won't get sick."

As much as I didn't want to get sick, I'd risk it to be in Walker's arms in that moment. I needed to feel like I was making the right decision and I couldn't do that if I was a few feet away from him.

No, I need him just as much as he needed me.

I only hoped I wouldn't regret letting him in because I knew if I lost Walker again, I would never be the same.

CHAPTER SEVENTEEN

walker

PEN PACED OUTSIDE the green room. For the last ten minutes, I couldn't take my eyes off her as she talked animatedly on the phone.

"Who's she talking to?" Kenton leaned in and quietly asked as if he was afraid Pen might hear him.

"Did we do something wrong?" Cross asked. His eyes flicked towards Greer.

"I didn't do a damn thing, asshole," Greer growled from where he was perched on the edge of the couch. He huffed and stood. "Why do we have to wait in here for her? Let's go to the bus. It's bigger than this shit hole room they gave us."

Kenton patted Greer on the shoulder. "One day it's going to be us who gets the big room. You just wait and see."

"You can go if you want to, but I'm going to stay here and walk her out. This isn't the best area for a woman to be walking alone at night." I leaned back and made myself comfortable.

"Oh, come on, Walker." Greer let out a humorless laugh. "The bus is probably parked a whole five feet away from the back door. She can make the short trip on her own."

Narrowing my eyes, I landed them on him and let him feel the heat of my words. "I never said she couldn't, but I'm not going to risk it. You can be an asshole and not wait."

We always waited for Pen before we headed out or at least until she dismissed us. Usually, she gave the guys time to get their fuck on with whatever groupie they picked for the night.

"You're the asshole, but of course, no one is going to call you out on it," Greer shot back as he pushed out the door.

I looked to both Kenton and Cross to see if they had any clue what that was about, but they both shrugged with confused expressions on their faces.

Cross stood next and gave me an uneasy smile. "I'm sure she's going to want to go once she's off the phone. Maybe I'll just slip into the bathroom and get some head before we're trapped on the bus for the rest of the night."

"Do what you got to do." I was sure I'd feel the same way if I didn't have Pen on the bus with me. I was probably the one getting the least action out of the four of us, though. The bus was small, and sound carried, making it difficult to please my woman whenever I wanted. She was a little loud in the sack, but I wouldn't have it any other way. I liked hearing all the sounds she made as I touched her and the way she called out my name as she came around my dick.

Fuck we really needed a night at a hotel and quick.

"Oh, my God," Pen shouted as she stepped into the room. "You're never going to believe what just happened!"

"We just sold a million copies of our album?" Cross guessed.

"Not that," Pen shook her head. The biggest smile I'd ever seen was plastered on her face.

"Don't keep us guessing. Tell us what it is," I demanded.

"Okay, okay," she surveyed the room once and then twice. "Where's Greer?"

"He went to the bus. Said he couldn't wait any longer," Cross said irritably.

"Well, he's going to want to hear this, so let's go." She grabbed my hand and helped me to stand. Well, it was the thought that counted. She couldn't pull me up even if she wanted to. Hooking both of her arms through Cross and

Kenton's, Pen started to pull them out of the room, skipping down the hallway.

"Whatever this is, it must be good," Kenton laughed.

"It's so fucking good you're going to shit your pants," Pen laughed.

Now I was intrigued. What could possibly have her acting like we'd just won an Oscar for best musical score or gone platinum on our first album?

Walking behind them, I watched as Pen's ass moved in her tight jeans as she skipped and dragged the guys down the hall. It was quite a sight. Her mood was infectious, and had put smiles on all of our faces. Not that I wasn't usually in a good mood when she was around. Pen made my world better, even if we were hiding what we meant to each other from the world.

Pen let go of their arms and ran up the stairs of the bus with all of us hot on her heels.

"Okay, now that you're all together, I have big news to share with you. What would you say if I told you, you've just been offered to do an international tour with Crimson Heat as…"

My heart nearly pumped out of my chest as I listened to each of her words. Time slowed down as I waited to hear what else she had to say.

"The headlining band." Pen jumped up and down in place and clapped her hands.

The rest of us just stood there in stunned silence, not believing the words that just came out of her mouth.

"You've got to be shitting me," Cross yelled before he picked Penelope up and twirled her around.

Kenton got in on the action as well. They held Pen up and made small circles in our little home away from home. With each spin, Pen's eyes locked with mine. There was nothing I wanted more than to hold her in my arms and kiss her. Instead, all I could do was smile at my bandmates, friends, and the woman I loved.

Yeah, I loved her. I thought I was already halfway there when she ended things, but once she curled up against me and cried in my lap, I knew I loved her. Which was something I was keeping to myself for the time being. I didn't want to rock the boat and make Pen second guess what was going on between us. I knew if I told her right then and there, she wouldn't believe me, but soon I'd tell her. There was no way in hell I could keep my feelings contained any longer. The second we were alone, I was going to tell Pen I loved her.

"I fucking love this woman," Kenton crowed, saying to the bus and the world what I wanted to say. I knew his feelings were strictly platonic, but still, it ate away at me that I couldn't even show these three guys how I felt about her.

They put Pen down on her feet, and she stumbled

dizzily into my arms. She braced her hands on my chest and smiled up at me. The look she was giving me had me second-guessing if she had indeed been dizzy or not. I had a feeling she just wanted to be in my arms. Pen patted my chest, right over my heart. Her eyes closed for a moment, and then she was spinning around and smiling at all of us.

"Give us all the details, woman. When? Where? For how long?" Kenton rushed out.

"How much are we making?"

"I don't have all the details yet, but I should have an email soon with all the locations, dates, venues, and more. But so far, this is what I know."

For the next ten minutes, Pen filled us in on everything she learned while she was talking on the phone out in the hall. By the end, the four of us were about to jump out of our skin with excitement. You could feel a crackle in the air. We couldn't be contained.

"Alright, I'm going to check to see how long it will take us to get to your next city. You guys need to go out and celebrate. Otherwise, you'll probably tear down the bus with all of your energy."

She wasn't wrong. It looked like it was taking everything in Kenton to not be bouncing off the walls.

Pen stood, pulled out her phone, and walked to the back of the bus as she tried to figure out what she should do with us.

After a minute, I feigned the need to use the restroom and followed her to the back of the bus. I closed the curtains at the bunks so no one could see that I didn't go inside the bathroom. I found Pen sitting on the bed, looking down at her phone, her brows pinched.

I leaned against the door frame, taking her in. "Hey, pretty lady. How's it going?"

Her head popped up, and she laughed. "Is that your pickup line? Because if that's the case, you need to work on it. You'll never get a girl with a line like that."

I hummed as I stalked closer to her. "I don't need lines. See, I got the girl that I wanted without one and I don't plan to ever let her go. So lame or not, I think I'm good."

"That you are Mr. Pierce. I do have to say if you had tried using something lame like that on me, it wouldn't have worked for you. In fact, it might have hindered your chances even more."

Placing my hand over my heart, I gasped at her in mock horror. "You wound me with your words."

"Doubtful. You're pretty cocky." She looked back down at her phone screen.

I palmed said cock and wiggled my eyebrows at her. "You know how cocky I really am. Do I live up to the hype?"

"You more than live up to it. That's why I've been spreading rumors of your small dick at every show, so the women will stay away from you." She rolled her lips to keep from laughing.

Tilting my head back, I laughed, knowing she was fucking with me. I knew Pen didn't like even the thought of seeing women hitting on me, but I knew she'd never stoop so low as to put down my dick.

Pen looked in the direction of where I'd left the guys and held her hand out for me. In one stride, I had her smooth hand in mind. "Are you happy?"

"I can count the number of times I've been happier on one hand, so yeah," I answered her, kissing her.

"And what times would those be?" She asked breathily.

"The night you touched yourself in my room, the first time you let me inside your slick heat, the day we signed our contract, and the day you took me back. Well, that day is numero uno. At least for now."

"You think there will be others that trump today?" Pen pulled me closer until I was standing between her legs. Her hands ran up the outside of my thighs before her fingers hooked into the loops on my jeans.

"Oh, I know there will, and they'll all involve you," I confessed. I was picturing the day I asked her to marry me, and the day we got married, the world knew she was mine.

"Do you plan to keep me around after you're big and famous?"

"My sweet, sweet Penny. I'm going to keep you around

for as long as I live. You just wait and see." I leaned down and nipped her bottom lip. "Pen, I l— "

"Yo, get your ass out here, man," Cross shouted.

Pen let out a shakily laugh. "Until later. Let's go. I want to talk to you all about what we can do tonight."

I pulled her up and pressed my body into her letting her feel how much I wanted her. "As long as I can be with you, I don't care what we do."

"Well," she laughed. "I have a feeling the rest of the guys won't feel the same way."

"That's because they're a bunch of assholes." I nipped at her bottom lip and then sucked on it before pulling away, knowing that at any moment, we would be interrupted if we didn't get out there.

"That's not true. They're just not sleeping with me."

"And that's a damn good thing. Otherwise, I'd have to kill them. Hell, I fantasize about it every time I see them look at you with anything not akin to how they'd look at their sister."

"Alright, Mr. Alpha. Cool your jets." Lifting up on her toes, Pen placed the softest of kisses on my desperate lips. "Congratulations, Walker. I'm so happy for you."

Fuck, I was done for. Pen was made for me. Here she was getting us an international tour and congratulating us when it should have been the other way around.

"Alright, boys," Pen said as she made her way through

the curtain. "Unfortunately, our next city is eight hours away. We were planning on heading there right away, but I think you need a night to celebrate. So, what do you say we stay here tonight? You can go out, and I'll try to find a hotel with a vacancy big enough for the staff."

"I think this is why we love you. You're the fucking best, Pen." Kenton rushed her and hugged Pen to his tall frame.

"Ah, you're going to make me cry. I'm just doing my job." She patted Kenton on the back.

"Yeah, that may be so, but you're going above and beyond because you care. If we had Cristiano as our manager, he'd have us on the road wishing we had someone to suck our dicks."

Pen pushed away and laughed. "Okay, that's more than I need to know. Why don't you guys find someplace you want to go while I work on hotel accommodations?"

Leaning down, I made sure no one could hear me as I said. "Make sure our rooms are right next to each other. Better yet, get ones that are connected because I'm planning to be inside of you for the rest of the night."

Pen bit her bottom lip as she nodded. "I'll see what I can do."

"Make sure that you do."

I sat down, discreetly adjusting myself in my pants. I couldn't wait to celebrate inside my sweet Pen.

CHAPTER EIGHTEEN

pen

BEING at a club while I watched countless women throw themselves at my… man? Boyfriend? Lover? Boy Toy? I had no idea what to call Walker except the best sex of my life and someone I was falling deeper and deeper for with each passing day.

The problem was exactly what was happening at that very moment. Walker couldn't push every woman away that came onto him, nor could he be with me each second when the guys were around. Still, it was unreal how no one could feel the laser beams shooting out of my eyes at the women who could touch him when I couldn't.

I wanted to eviscerate every single one of them, but instead, I had to pretend I didn't wish death to seventy percent of the people in the club. It was a very good thing I didn't have to pretend to be having a good time because my acting skills were not on that level. No, I was doing my job, and that was to make sure the guys didn't get into any fights or do anything towards anyone that could be considered sexual harassment. Because unfortunately, there were too many people out there who were looking for a quick buck, and nothing was easier than hitting on a guy who was rising to success, getting him to touch you, only to say it wasn't consensual, and then suing him.

Kenton sidled in next to me and threw his arm around my shoulders. "Why so glum, Pen?"

"I'm not glum." I tilted my head at an uncomfortable angle to be able to look at his face. He was so damn tall. "How tall are you?"

A goofy smile took over as he looked down at me. "I can't believe it took you this long to ask. Normally it's the first thing anyone asks me."

"What can I say? I'm not a normal kind of girl," I laughed.

"No, you're not. You're heads above the rest of them." He leaned against the wall making it, so he wasn't towering over me. "I'm six ten."

"I was going to guess seven feet. I don't think I've ever met anyone as tall as you. Are your parents tall?"

He barked out a laugh, but I didn't see what was so funny. "It's a running joke that my mom slept with the mailman because my dad is barely five ten, and my mom is five-foot-two."

My mouth fell open. "Is—"

"No, truth to it," Kenton stopped me from what I was about to ask. "There are some tall family members a couple of generations back on both sides, and I guess I got it from them," he shrugged as if it was no big deal. Surely, it wasn't fun for your mom to be the brunt of the joke that she cheated on his dad.

"Now, what's eating you? We're all being good except for drinking too much."

"Drinking can lead to behavior that can get you in trouble," I reminded him. "But nothing's wrong. I just have a lot of things on my mind now that you're going worldwide."

"I keep pinching myself, thinking it's a dream, but each time, it hurts like hell." He pinched his arm and grimaced.

"It's real, and you all deserve it. I'm so proud of all of you. You each pour your heart and soul out each night, and it shows. Fans love your music. I don't think it will be long until you're a household name. I bet one of your songs will be in a commercial in a year."

"Are you serious?" Kenton swayed on his feet, his face in shock and wonder.

"I don't joke about business, and I wouldn't say anything if I didn't believe it," I promised him.

"Fucking hell," he said, barely more than a whisper. Gripping my arm, he turned to face me. "If you're okay, I'm going to get out there and celebrate how awesome my life is."

"I'm more than okay, Kenton. Thank you for checking in on me." I patted his hand that was still on my arm. "Go have fun."

I'd barely gotten the words out before he was getting lost in the crowd. At least, he'd gotten my mind off of Walker. The reprieve was nice, no matter how short it might have been.

Pulling out my phone, I checked my email again to see if Cristiano had sent anything about the new tour. Never before had I been so happy to have some work to do. Opening up the email, I was shocked to see how many countries Crimson Heat would be playing in. The tour was going to last for four months, and he hadn't scheduled much of a break for them between opening for Tragic Phenomenon and the new one. I growled in frustration. There was a lot of work I needed to do and not a lot of time.

With no time like the present, I started making plans, booking hotel rooms, plane tickets, buses, vans, and a thousand other things being on an international tour entailed. Even as I worked on my phone, I kept my eye on Walker, or should I say the women around him.

My back stiffened as a busty redhead ran her red-tipped fingernails up Walker's chest and wrapped her other hand around his neck, trying to pull him down to her.

My vision turned red. I was surprised by how hard I was clutching my phone and the fact that I didn't break it. Standing abruptly from the stool I was perched on, I walked to the front door, and the second I was outside, I took in a breath like I'd been holding it since I saw that woman touching Walker.

I moved by the crowd and down the sidewalk until I was far enough away, I couldn't hear what anyone was saying. Resting the back of my head against the cool brick surface, I closed my eyes and tried to wipe away the images I'd just seen.

"Hey." Strong and familiar arms pulled me into a hard chest that smelled of the breeze coming off the sea and smoke. I could have done without the latter as I buried my head between Walker's pecs and sighed. "What are you doing out here?"

I trailed my hands down his back and rested my hands in the pockets of his dark jeans for only a moment before I pulled away and put some distance between us when I remembered there was an entire line of people who could see us only a handful of feet away.

Walker looked down at me with heavily furrowed brows. "What's going on?"

I tipped my head toward the crowd and raised an eyebrow. Need I say more? What the hell was he thinking?

"I came outside to get some air. What are you doing out here?" I was sure the guys were wondering why he was not inside getting felt up.

"I followed you out when I saw you looked upset." He moved to reach for me but dropped his hand. A deep frown formed before he demanded, "Tell me what's really going on."

Looking toward the door in case any of the other guys came out, or so I was telling myself, was the reason I couldn't look at him, as I spoke with my hands clenched at my sides. "I didn't like seeing all those women touching you."

"And I didn't like them touching me." Reaching up, he tucked a strand of hair behind my ear. His fingers lingered a little longer than was required. I wanted so badly to lean into his touch, but I fought the urge. "The whole time, I was imagining it was you."

"That doesn't make me feel any better," I whispered, trying like hell to hide the hurt in my tone. Hiding what Walker was coming to mean to me was slowly killing me. I wasn't sure how long we could last this way.

"Hey, it won't be this way forever, and soon we'll be able to stay in the same hotel room."

"We'll still have to hide it, but yeah, we should be able

to stay the night with each other more than the occasional one we get now. I don't like this sneaking around. I feel like we're seconds away from getting caught with each passing day."

"I know, Pen, I do, but I can't let you go. When we weren't together, it was like my world had become a black hole, and I don't want to go back to that." Ducking his head down until he was eye level with me, I was taken aback by the turmoil that was swirling in his charcoal eyes. "Tell me that's not what you want."

"It's not what I want," I whispered into the night, hoping the wind would hear the plea in my words and nothing bad would come of us.

"Alright," he nodded. "I'm going to go back inside and try to wrangle the guys. I've had enough of this place."

He moved to step away, but I caught his arm. "They're not going to want to leave."

"Maybe not, but I'll tell them I'm not feeling well or whatever it takes to get them to leave. Why don't you call us a car, and I'll be back in a minute?"

It wasn't easy finding an Uber that would fit all of us at one in the morning, but I managed. I watched on the app as the car got closer with no sign of the guys. A sigh of relief left me when I saw Walker come striding out until I saw he was alone. His steps were heavy as he walked toward me.

"Those assholes aren't coming," he gritted out, nostrils flaring. "You go on and head back to the hotel, and I'll make sure they behave."

"I can't ask you to do my job." I didn't want to start down this slippery slope of Walker doing things for me because he was my... whatever he was. Turning to him, I meant to tell him we should go back inside. Instead, I said the one thing that was on my mind right at that moment. "What are we?"

Walker cocked his head, gazing down at me, and blinked a few times. "What do you mean, what are we?"

Oh God, did he really have no clue, or did he just want to hear the words come out of my mouth?

"What are we to each other? Are we lovers, friends with benefits, or...?"

Walker growled, clasping my hand in his and dragging me to where no one could see us from the side of the nightclub, and then pressed me up against the wall. "While yes, we *are* lovers, I seriously hope you were only kidding about the friends with benefits things."

"Well, you didn't let me finish talking before you went all alpha on me, growled, and dragged me away. I was thinking about this earlier. I don't know what to call you."

"Are you telling anyone about us?"

"I'm going to tell Stella. I plan to see her before we leave the country. I haven't seen her in person in forever, and now that she's finished moving, I'm going to see her."

His hand clasped my jaw with his thumb rubbing along the edge as he pressed every fine inch of his body to mine. "I like that you want to tell her. Tell Stella I'm your boyfriend."

"But are you my boyfriend?"

"Yes, my sweet Penny, I'm your fucking boyfriend" Leaning down, his mouth brushed across my lips that were desperate to feel his on mine. "It doesn't matter that we can't shout it from the rooftops. You're mine in every way that matters." He finished off with a nip to my bottom lip and then sucked.

"Are you mine?" I panted, desperate to be alone with Walker. I wanted for us to be back in our hotel room where he could show me how he felt.

"I've been yours since the day we met. You have nothing to worry about, Pen. You own me." There was a slight pause as if he wanted to say more, but instead, Walker looked heatedly down at my lips like he wanted to consume me.

Giving him what he wanted, I crashed my mouth to his, and threaded my fingers through his hair, and pulled him closer. Walker licked along the seam of my lips, and I happily opened for him. I needed him the same way he needed me. With each caress of our tongues, the night faded away until all thoughts of work and the women inside were forgotten. I drank in everything he gave me, and when we broke apart at the sound of a loud noise, we were both panting with need.

"We need to get the guys and get out of here because I plan to do wicked things to that body of yours." Each word was deep and gravelly, with a more pronounced rasp than usual, sending tingles down my spine.

"You read my mind."

CHAPTER NINETEEN

walker

PULLING Penelope tighter into my body, I glared at the group of hipsters who just looked her up and down like she was their own personal snack.

Maybe going to the Red Light district wasn't the best idea. While it was fascinating, I couldn't drag Pen into any of the shops or pin her up against one of the windows and take her from behind for anyone and everyone to see.

Lexie, Pen and Stella's friend, looked at everything with bright eyes and enthusiasm while Stella looked like she'd rather be anywhere else.

"Let's go in here," Lexie pulled Stella into what looked like a strip club with me and Pen hot on their heels. After paying the cover, we walked into a room lit by a blacklight, with at least fifty people scattered around tables near the stage of women dancing with glow-in-the-dark-painted bodies.

"I wish I had my camera," Lexie sighed. "Not that they'd let me take their pictures, but this is beautiful."

"Will Ryder not care you're here?" Pen asked as we sat down at a circular booth that faced the stage. She curled her hand around the inside of my thigh as she faced her friends. I liked that we could be a couple in front of someone, and it had me longing for whenever we'd have the opportunity in our future to be out to the world.

"Ryder?" Lexie smiled and shook her head. "No, he won't care. Now, it would be different if we went into one of those rooms back there. He might be jealous he wasn't here to experience it with me, but I'll remedy that by bringing him here and having a little fun for ourselves when we do."

Leaning over, I brush my lips to the shell of Pen's ear. "I wish I could take you into one of those rooms."

The grip on my thigh tightened as her lust-filled eyes met mine. "What would you do to me?"

"First, we have to imagine you're in a short little skirt and that I'd let anyone watch me touch you. Your pleasure is for me and me alone. After walking into that cubicle for all to see, I'd push you up against the window and flip your skirt up. Slowly I'd slip your underwear down those toned stems of yours. I'd keep them at your ankles and make you spread your legs as wide as they'd go. My tongue would follow my hands trailing up the inside of your thighs. Once I reached your core, I'd run my tongue front to back, spearing deep inside your wetness because I know you'd be wet for me just like you are now. Are you wet for me, my sweet Pen?"

Resting her head on my shoulder, Pen panted out her breathy one-word reply into my neck. "Yes."

"That's what I thought. Standing up, I'd slap that perfect ass of yours until it was nice and pink for letting anyone see how you look when you're turned on. Pulling out my dick, I would slam into you so hard you'd have to catch your breath. Gripping your hip with one hand, I'd hold you by the throat with the other and pound into you relentlessly only to slow down when you're close to coming. I'd repeat that over and over again until you begged for me to let you come. Pressing my front to your back, I would bury myself deep inside of you and then slap your pussy, making you come all over my dick which in turn sets me off. Slowly, I'd thrust in and out as you milk my cock, and only once I'm drained do I turn you around and take your mouth with my tongue. I would fuck your mouth like I fucked that sweet as sin pussy until we're both breathless."

"Oh, my fucking God, where did you say you found him again? That was some straight-up porn right there," Lexie giggled.

It was hard to break away from Pen panting against my neck like I'd just done everything I'd described to her to look across the table.

"I think I need a cold shower after hearing that." Stella's eyes widened as she leaned toward us. "Can I use that in one of my books?"

"Feel free. Consider it payment for posting about Crimson Heat on your Instagram profiles."

Earlier, when we were eating, both Lexie and Stella said they'd post about the band on their social media accounts. Lexie was going to have her husband, who had over a million followers, post about us as well. She said he had the right demographic, which was young women thirsting after hot guys, and they'd eat us up.

"Are you guys up for getting a drink before we head back to the hotel?" Lexie smirked at us.

"Yeah," Pen sat up and cleared her throat. "I want to spend as much time with you guys as I can since it will be a few months before I see you again."

Even though I knew Pen missed her best friend, I only wanted to drag her away from the table and to our hotel room where we could recreate what I'd just described to her. But I knew I'd be seeing my girl every day for the next three months while Pen only had tonight with Stella and Lexie.

Slouching down in the booth, I adjusted myself under

the table. I didn't want the girls to see my hard-on through my pants. I couldn't stop picturing all the dirty things I could do in one of the rooms along the district with Pen if I had the chance.

Pen leaned over with a wicked smile on her face. It made me wonder if she was thinking of all the different ways I could pleasure her if I had the chance, too. "You need to stop thinking whatever it is you're thinking," she giggled. "I'm not going to be able to spend any time with my friends if all I want to do is jump you."

Resting my arms along the top of the booth, I let one hand fall down to play with her hair. "I can't help it that I'm irresistible."

"Oh God, please." She leaned into me. I loved that she had no problem showing her affection for me in front of her friends. Earlier in the night, I'd been wary of what the protocol was going to be, but with each passing minute with her friends, I could feel both our guards slowly coming down. "I do not need you to be any cockier than you already are. Just behave. Please."

Pressing my mouth to hers, I spoke against her pink pouty lips. "I'll see what I can do."

For the next hour, we sat and watched some of the best strippers I'd ever seen dance on stage while their bodies glowed under the black lights overhead. None of them turned me on like they usually would. No, I had a feeling the only person who could do that now was the woman sitting at my side with a happy smile on her face as she and her friends chatted and watched the show while drinking their glasses of wine.

"Alright," Lexie stood, and everyone else at the table stood along with her. "I think we've put him through enough torture for one night. Let's head back to the hotel."

After taking an Uber back to the hotel, we said our goodbyes to Stella and Lexie outside their room which was a few floors above ours.

"When you get back from the tour, why don't we set up a photoshoot for the band? We can even do it at my house. We can have a barbecue and hang around the pool. It will be super casual, and I'll take pictures."

Pen gave Lexie a big hug. "That would be amazing. Thank you. I'll definitely do that."

Pen and Stella hugged for a long while, whispering words back and forth to each other. A few times, they'd look at me and then giggle. I was glad Pen didn't have to feel guilty anymore about hiding our relationship from her best friend. I knew Stella probably thought I was all wrong for her friend, but maybe after tonight, I'd get her seal of approval.

Stella and Pen broke apart both with tears in their eyes as they said goodbye. Pen snuggled up to my side as we walked back to the elevator. Once inside, I wiped away her tears that had fallen as we walked and kissed her salty lips.

"It won't be long until you see her again."

"I know, and I'm lucky they came all this way to see me for one night. With the time differences, it's been hard to keep in contact with her."

We stood in the middle of the elevator with me holding her, swaying back and forth to the elevator music until the elevator stopped. Then we went back to being the band member and manager walking with at least a couple of feet between us.

Stopping outside her door, Pen used her keycard to open it. Once she stepped inside, she looked up at me from underneath her eyelashes and fluttered them at me. "Give me two minutes, and then come into my room."

I licked my lips, hungry for her. This was going to be the longest two minutes of my life. Going inside my room next to hers, I stripped as I walked to the door that connected our rooms together. My door was already open and when I reached the entrance, so was hers.

Before me, Pen had already removed all of her clothes, and she was spread across the bed, biting her bottom lip. I didn't think she had any idea how seductive she looked right then.

I stalked into the room and crawled onto the bed,

hovering above her. Pen ran her hands down my chest, circled my cock with her fingers, and started stroking me.

Pushing up onto her elbows, Pen ran her tongue up my neck and nipped my chin. "I want you to do me what you described earlier against that window." She looked to her right at the big window that overlooked Amsterdam.

Kissing between her breasts and down her taut stomach, I ran my hands down her ribs. Moving down further, I skimmed my nose through her slit, knowing I'd soon have my tongue deep inside of her. I stood at the end of the bed and took her in, relishing the fact that Penelope was mine. I wanted to claim her and for everyone to know who she belonged to.

Gripping her by the ankle, I pulled her to the end of the bed and then up against my body. My cock was trapped between us, pre-cum already leaking out at the thought of what I was going to do to her. "Let me show you my fantasy."

CHAPTER TWENTY

pen

WE WERE WALKING along the sidewalk of the small village of Oia, Greece, when Kenton stopped dead in his tracks and doubled over in laugher.

"We've got to go in here," he sputtered out, pointing to the window of one of the shops that lined the street.

Walker, who was at the other end of our Crimson Heat parade from me, moved toward a still laughing Kenton. It was difficult to keep our distance on days like today. We had a day off today, and we decided to go sightseeing in the small town on the coast. When we decided to come here for the day, I had no idea we'd be trekking down streets and sidewalks with deep slopes that would have my calves burning with exertion. Even with how exhausted I was, the water and town were beautiful. All I wanted to do was hold Walker's hand as we navigated one of the most beautiful places we'd been so far on tour, maybe kiss him every once in a while, but that was not going to happen with everyone around us. Still, I was happy to be here with them.

"Wow, I've never seen so many peni," Cross cocked his head to the side and scrunched his nose. "Is peni the plural for penis?" He shook his head and laughed. "I've never seen so many of them all in one place."

"I know," Kenton laughed. "We have to go in."

They truly were boys sometimes, and right then was one of the times.

I stood back and watched as four hulking men walked inside this little shop. Once we were all inside, it felt like there was hardly any space left for us to move. First to catch my eye were these dildo-like bottle openers that ranged in size and color. There were flesh-colored ones, and then there were ones that were striped like a rainbow, green, red, blue, and teal with flowers painted on them. A particularly large teal one caught my eye. Did women use these to pleasure themselves?

"Damn, Pen, you like them large, huh?" Kenton laughed when he saw me holding the wooden bottle opener.

"You know the saying, go big or go home. That's how I like my men," I laughed along with him, keeping my teal penis to buy. This was the best damn souvenir I'd ever found. I picked up an orange and rainbow one for Lexi and Stella, along with a few keychains. I figured they'd get a kick out of them, at least.

"This is the best shop ever." Kenton grabbed a handful of tiny chocolate penises. "We've got to take a picture of us eating these and post it."

"If you were a zombie and ate a dick, would that make you gay?" Cross asked with a wicked grin.

"Eating chocolate dick doesn't make you gay, so I say no," Kenton answered back without missing a beat.

Boys.

I chuckled to myself as I walked through the shop. A little old lady was behind the counter, probably wishing we'd leave before we broke something—or everything.

"I'm getting these," Cross said giddily. I looked up to find him with a hand-size penis soap in each hand, caressing them up and down his cheeks. "There's something about bathing with penis-shaped soap that I like."

At that point, I couldn't control my laughter. Even Greer cracked a smile at Cross rubbing them on his face, making an 'O' with his mouth and moaning.

With the shop owner watching them with a bored expression, all four boys started rubbing themselves all over while they made the most provocative noises I'd ever heard from most of them. With Walker, I was very well acquainted with the noises he made, and I loved how he would groan and growl when he came. Luckily, he wasn't doing that now because I wasn't sure I'd be able to control myself.

To clear my head of thoughts I shouldn't be having, I moved to the side of the shop that didn't have any penis paraphernalia.

Walker appeared beside me, catching me off guard. He could be sneaky when he had to, which was quite often lately. Looking down at me, he smirked. "We'll be lucky to get out of here without at least one of everything."

"That's fine. I've got my share of penis fun. I think all of this would be great gag gifts for the girls, and maybe one of these can keep me company when you can't." I wagged the long penis bottle opener at him.

The smirk he was wearing quickly faded from his face. "That's not even funny. When have I ever left you hanging? We don't have to spend a night alone this entire tour."

True.

Turning, I looked around to make sure no one would be able to hear me and then asked. "Are you saying we couldn't have a little fun with one of these?"

Gripping me by the arm, Walker took my loot and set it down on the counter before pulling me out onto the sidewalk. He loomed over me, his dark eyes swimming with lust. "If you want to play, I'm happy to play, baby. I've got all kinds of things I want to do to you."

My breath hitched as my pulse sky-rocketed. My thoughts raced to how long it would be until we were alone back in our hotel room. With the way I was feeling, I'd be happy with a little side alley action. Maybe we could sneak into a bathroom during lunch.

Walker's hand gripped my hip as he leaned down. "I don't know what you're thinking, but I like it. Don't worry, my lucky Penny, I'll find a way for us to be alone."

It was like he could read my mind. Maybe he could smell how wet I was for him.

"Lucky Penny? That's new," I tossed over my shoulder as I walked inside the shop.

"That's because ever since I met you, I've been lucky, and I think it's because of you."

Damn, he was sweet.

Now I wanted to find a dark place to be alone with him even more.

I blew him a kiss before I schooled my features. "Have you guys got everything you want to buy? I'm getting hungry."

One of the things we weren't expecting for the whole town to pretty much shut down for a couple of hours in the afternoon. I could get on board with a place that stopped so you could take a nap every day, but damn, was I hungry.

"I'm fucking starving," Greer grumbled as he walked past.

Cross nodded as his stomach made a loud noise. "All that walking has my stomach feeling like it might start eating itself."

Boys could be so dramatic.

"Alright, let's buy our goodies and get out of this poor woman's hair." I smiled at the lady, who kindly smiled back.

"I bet we're her best customers of the day," Kenton said as he dumped a pile of penis—well, everything—onto the countertop.

We probably were.

While the rest checked out, I went and got some chocolate and soap penises because a girl needed to have fun. Maybe if Stella got married one day, I could give her these at her bridal shower. Who was I kidding? I'd be lucky to wait until her birthday. I'd probably give them to her the first time I saw her.

After buying a plethora of penises, we headed down the street in search of some lunch. We found a cute little restaurant with a courtyard where we could sit outside and enjoy the breeze and sunshine. It was nice to feel the sun on my skin after endless days of being stuck on a bus or plane.

The walls and tables were cream with seafoam green painted chairs. There were terra cotta planters with different plants sprinkled around the courtyard, having a calming effect on me.

We all sat around a table looking at menus. It was impossible to pick what I wanted to eat. Everything looked good. It didn't help that we were all starving.

"When I retire in our very distant future, I want to live here," Walker muttered from next to me.

"It is beautiful. One day of being here isn't enough."

Walker's hand gripped my thigh under the table and squeezed. Leaning over, he spoke quietly enough for only me to hear. "What about a lifetime?"

I liked that Walker thought about us in the long term. He wasn't your typical twenty-one-year-old guy. If he was, I didn't think I'd find him so attractive. He was serious about himself, his career, and his band—all things I loved. And most importantly, Walker was serious about us.

Reaching over, I squeezed his hand under the table. What I wouldn't give to hold his hand for all to see. "I could live with that."

"Only just live? I think you can do better than that."

"We'll have to see." I cleared my throat. "Has everyone

else figured out what they want? Because I feel like I want one of everything."

"Why don't we get a bunch of different items and share?" Cross suggested.

I pointed at him. "I like the way you think." Pulling out my company credit card, I flashed it. "Plus, it's on Titan Records, so let's splurge."

"Oh, hell, yeah," Cross cheered. "Why don't we do this more often?"

"Because I want to keep my job, and the tour needs to be profitable," I laughed. There was no way we could spend more money than the tour was making by eating out, but that was a small expense. It was the hotels and flights, along with the crew, that ate up the profits. It was a good thing everyone was loving Crimson Heat and was buying their songs and selling out venues over here in Europe.

Cross shrugged, setting down his menu. "I guess that makes sense. I don't know what we'd do without you."

"Oh, please," Greer rolled his eyes. "You act like she's done all of this out of the kindness of her heart. She's making money off us. You don't think she'd drop us if we weren't bringing in the green."

I wanted to reach across the table and slap him a couple of times. When was Greer going to finally give me a chance?

"You need to shut your mouth before I do it for you," Walker growled out. "Pen has fought to give us everything we have, and here you sit like some ungrateful asshole."

Greer scooted back. The legs of the chair scraping against the ground made the most god-awful screeching sound. It was worse than nails on a chalkboard. "I don't have to put up with this shit. You all can kiss her ass all day and all night for all I care, but I'm done."

Greer stalked away, not turning back as Cross and Kenton called after him. His only response was to flip them off.

"So much for having a nice meal," Kenton grumbled.

Cross scoffed, "How about so much for having a nice day without Greer being an asshole?"

Hanging my head, I closed my eyes and sighed. "He's free to have his own opinion on me." I looked up and tried to smile at them. "But thank you for what you said. It means a lot to me, and I want you to know you feel like family to me."

"So," Kenton drew out the word. "Does that mean if Walker ever gets to fuck you, it will be like incest?"

"Kenton," Walker barked out. "Not today."

Kenton held his hands up as his face fell. Seeing him like that didn't seem right. I loved that Kenton was always so happy. "I'm sorry. I was trying to lighten the mood, not make it worse."

"Why don't we all get a drink as well and try to relax. Let's forget about Greer. He probably got his dick stuck up his ass or something and is extra pissy today. The one thing I do know is I'm not going to let him ruin Greece for me."

"You don't have to act like it doesn't bother you," Walker started as I shook my head.

"Not everyone has to like me, and that's fine," I tried to assure them all.

Luckily our waiter came, and we ordered our drinks and food, ending our talk about Greer. He was close to ruining our time, but I wouldn't let him. Not now. Not ever.

"Okay, boys, do you all think you can behave while I go to the bathroom?"

Their only answer was to either flip me off or roll their eyes. I mean, how much trouble could they get into? There was only one other group at the restaurant, and they were seated on the other side of the courtyard from us.

I'd barely closed the door to the bathroom before it opened, and Walker slid inside the room. He closed and locked the door, and when he turned back around, his dark eyes immediately landed on my mouth.

I couldn't stop the smile that stretched across my face as I asked. "What are you doing in here?"

"I couldn't pass up the opportunity to be alone with you even if it was only for a moment."

Walker strode toward me like a man on a mission—and he was. Grabbing me by the waist, Walker moved me until I was caged against the door. His tongue slipped inside and swirled around mine. We both moaned as if it had been months since we last touched each other instead of a matter of hours.

Breaking away, Walker slid his hands up my neck and cupped the sides of my face. "Have I told you how happy I am you wore a dress today?"

"And why is that?" I asked, leaning forward to brush my mouth to his.

"Easy access for what I'm about to do to you," he replied hungrily before he took my mouth in a searing kiss. One hand ran up my outer thigh as he hitched my right leg around his hip. Dipping down, Walker laid kisses along my collarbone and up the column of my neck. "Reach down and pull out my cock."

Happily, I did as I was ordered. There was something hot about a guy taking charge when it came to sex.

"Wrap your legs around my waist. Tight," Walker gritted out as he bent at the knees and pushed the crown of his cock against my entrance. "This is going to be fast."

There was nothing wrong with a little fast and dirty sex. I glanced around the bathroom for the first time to notice that the bathroom was the same colors as outside, cream and green, and it was clean. That made me feel better about the bathroom sex I was about to have, which was laughable since I had been thinking of alley sex only an hour ago.

"Fuck me, Walker." I pushed down as he ran his shaft through my slick folds, needing him inside of me.

With one arm clamped around my waist, Walker slammed into me in one long thrust. I'd wanted him for so long that my core contracted around him, ready to detonate at the first touch.

"I love your sweet pussy," he grated in my ear.

With his other hand pressed against the bathroom door, Walker reared back and impaled me with his cock. I gasped, holding onto his shoulders tighter.

Pressing his forehead to mine, Walker ran his nose along mine. "Why does it always feel like heaven when I'm inside of you?"

Because we were meant to be together, I wanted to say.

Tangling my fingers in his dark strands, I rode Walker as he plunged in and out of me. I was quickly climbing, and even though I knew we had to be fast, I wanted to remember this moment, the moment I realized how perfectly we fit together and how far I'd fallen for him.

That thought and Walker hitting my sweet spot sent me over the edge. Digging my fingers into Walker's shoulder, I held on for dear life as pleasure shot through my body. I could barely keep my eyes open as I watched the way

Walker's body moved. Even with clothes on, he was the hottest man to ever fuck me. The way his back muscles rippled underneath the fabric of his dark gray t-shirt. How hot his ass looked with his jeans pulled halfway down as he powered into me.

"One more," he growled out. His thumb found my clit and moved in the most delicious circles, making me explode all over again. "That's it. Milk my cock. Show me how good I make you feel."

Walker wrapped his arms around me and moved to the edge of the sink, where he held me as he stilled, pulsing and shooting off deep inside of me.

Holding me close, Walker nuzzled and placed feather-light kisses up and down the side of my neck.

I rested my forehead to his shoulder, willing my heart rate to slow. "We should get back."

He nodded but didn't move. "I know. Give me one more minute with it just being the two of us." His hand ran up my back, and he cupped the nape of my neck. "All day, I've wanted to get you alone. I wanted my hands on you. To be able to kiss you."

I smiled into his shoulder. "I know. I've wanted the same thing. Wishing I could hold your hand as we walked along with the water in our view or kiss you. This is a romantic town meant for two."

Pulling back, Walker cupped the side of my face and

ran his thumb across the apple of my cheek. "I meant what I said about living here one day. I'm not talking next year, but someday."

I giggled because this was Walker. He was so damn sweet to me. "We could come here on vacation. We don't have to live here. You might change your mind after traveling more."

"I won't change my mind." He was so determined, but I didn't understand why.

"How can you say that?"

"Because this place is special." He said, pulling me impossibly closer.

I couldn't disagree that it was special, but there were plenty of places that were special or would be.

"It is, but— "

"I love you, Pen, and I want to spend the rest of my life with you."

I wanted to respond, to react, but before I could open my mouth, someone pounded on the door. "Hurry up, you two. Our food is going to get cold," Cross shouted.

And what I didn't want to happen happened in that moment. My worst nightmare came to life.

CHAPTER TWENTY-ONE

walker

PENELOPE SHOOK beside me as we walked back to the table. I held her hand in mine and rubbed my thumb over the back of her trying to soothe her. "It's going to be okay."

"How can you say that?" She hissed.

I didn't know for sure, but Cross and Kenton were like brothers to me. Albeit brothers I'd never had since I was an only child, but they were my real family, and your real family didn't fuck you over.

Kenton had the widest smile I'd ever seen plastered on his face as we stepped up to the table. "Ah, there's the happy couple. Are you going sit down so we can eat, or are you just going to stand there and stare at us?"

I pulled out Pen's chair and waited for her to sit before

I took the seat beside her. She looked green and as if she was about ready to throw up at any moment. Taking her hand back in mine, I tried my best to let her know we were in this together. I was slightly worried she might call it off now that they knew. She hadn't said she loved me back in the bathroom, not that she had a chance before Cross knocked on the door. I narrowed my eyes at him, pissed he'd ruined the moment. Perhaps the bathroom wasn't the best place to profess my love to her. I had wanted to wait until we got back to the hotel, but the words slipped out of their own volition. I started to open my mouth to tell them they couldn't say anything, but Pen beat me to the punch.

"Please don't say anything," came out her small, tortured words.

Kenton scoffed while Cross looked personally affronted by her words.

Cross started piling his plate full of the food that had arrived while we'd been in the bathroom. Maybe our quickie wasn't so quick after all. "If we haven't said anything before, why would we start now?"

Pulling our joined hands onto the table, I leaned forward with my elbows anchoring me to the spot. "What do you mean by that?"

"Did you really think we didn't know?" Cross laughed before shoving a forkful of food in his mouth.

It made no sense. These guys didn't know how to keep their mouths shut about anything. "Why didn't you say something if you knew?"

"Because you obviously wanted to keep it a secret," Cross rolled his eyes at me like I was an idiot.

"Why do you think I made the comment about incest earlier?" Kenton said, looking back and forth between us. "If we're a happy family, it's with you as the dad and Pen as our MILF of a mom, of course."

"Don't even," I growled.

"Oh, this is going to be so fun," Kenton laughed, and Cross joined in.

"Does Greer know?" Pen asked quietly. She was still shaking by my side. Moving my chair closer to hers, I wrapped my arm around her and gave her a squeeze.

"Oh, if he knew, he would have let you know." Cross's mouth turned into a thin line. "It would be best if he never found out."

"Especially if you want to keep it a secret," Kenton chimed in.

"I don't want to lose my job, and if Cristiano finds out, then..." Tears welled up in her golden eyes as she looked around the table at all of us.

"You could end it," Cross threw out there as if there was even a possibility I would let Pen go.

"Not happening," I gritted out.

"As much as I like finally seeing you two together, how do you think this is going to work? She's our manager." Cross's face went soft as he looked over at Pen. "And don't take this the wrong way, but she's a lot older than you are."

"Don't remind me," Pen murmured under her breath at the same time I said, "I don't care about her age."

"Okay, that may be so, but again, I'm not trying to be mean. I'm only stating questions anyone would have. What about kids? We're going to be on the road for hopefully a lot of years, and when that time comes," he looked at Pen and frowned. "You won't be young."

Sitting back in her chair, Pen narrowed her eyes at Kenton and Cross. "How old do you think I am?" They both shrugged and looked at me as if I was going to tell them. "Yes, I can't deny I have thought about it. I hope you become wildly successful and with that means lots of time on the road, and by the time you're ready to settle down and have a life, my eggs will be old and dried up."

Kenton scrunched up his face. "Yikes, way to paint a graphic picture for us."

Forgetting the two assholes across from us, I turned to Pen. When I looked at her, the world fell away. We were the only two people on the planet. In the short amount of time we'd been together, she had become my everything. "Do you want kids?"

This time it was Pen's turn to shrug. "I mean, I'm not opposed to them. I never thought I'd meet a guy I'd want to settle down and have kids with, so I always assumed I'd eventually be a crazy cat lady."

I scanned over her face looking for some kind of tell. What did she want out of life? What did she want out of our life together? "And now, what do you see?"

"I see you up on stage and me cheering you on for the next two decades or so. As for kids, I'm not sure they're in the cards for me or us. They're really not conducive to the Rockstar life."

No, they really weren't. I couldn't imagine having to leave Pen at home to take care of a baby while I was on tour for months on end, and I also couldn't imagine having a baby on the bus with us. A child growing up on the road would be tough, and eventually, he or she would need to go to school.

"I can't ask you if you want kids because you're still young, and you might change your mind." Pen looked down at my clasped hand in hers. "What if you change your mind one day, and it's too late for me?"

That was a big what if, but one I needed to think about.

"According to you, we're going to be big, and with that comes lots of money, right? She nodded, her whiskey eyes looking troubled as she watched me. "If we're rich, then we can adopt or hire a surrogate if the time comes that we ever want children."

"Dude, you're signing away your life at twenty-one. Can you really say you want to spend the rest of your life with her?" Cross held his hands up. "I'm not saying Pen isn't great, but how do you know it will last?"

"Not that it's any of your business, but you can never know with one hundred percent certainty that anything is going to last. You have to put yourself out there and go along for the ride, and I'm putting myself all in." Even though I was answering Cross, I was looking at Penelope, letting her know just how serious I was. I had just professed my love for her in the bathroom, but she needed to know if the sadness in her eyes was anything to go by. "I would give up everything for you to be by my side."

Eyes and mouth downturned, she tried to smile but was unsuccessful. "You say that now, but it would kill me for you to regret me later because I won't be able to give you what you want."

"You could have a baby now," Kenton threw out there.

Looking away from Pen, I glared at Kenton. "That isn't the solution to any of our problems right now."

"Sorry, I can't believe we're here to witness this. It seems rather— "

"Personal," Pen said for him. "It is, but as I said earlier, you're family, and now that we don't have to hide our relationship from you, you might as well know how serious we are."

"And you're serious?" Kenton tilted his head to the side, waiting for our answer.

"So serious, I would marry her tomorrow."

"That's it," Kenton boomed out, causing everyone to look at us. "If you get married, there's no way Titan Records can fire you, and then you can be our manager forever."

What Kenton said did make sense.

I looked over at Pen. "What do you say? I know I only told you I love you today even though I think I've loved you since the moment I saw you."

One of the guys, I wasn't sure which one, but I think it was Kenton, made a long, drawn-out aww sound.

Pen bit her lip and then nodded. "What better way to spend our last night in Greece than getting married."

"Today?" I questioned. When I asked her, I hadn't thought of the logistics.

"We don't have another free day until the tour is almost over. It's either now or never."

"Wow, when you two go in, you go *all* in. We don't even have time to throw you a bachelor party. So, what's it going to be. I hate to break it to you, but time is ticking," Cross pointed out.

"You don't have to tell us. I don't even know where to

start with getting married tonight." Pen looked up to the sky and muttered a few words.

Gripping her chin with my thumb and forefinger, I pulled until her gaze met mine. "Hey, we don't have to do this now. It can wait until after the tour is over. I don't want to pressure you into doing anything you don't want to do."

I didn't even know if she loved me. I couldn't ask her to marry me and spend the rest of her life with me if she didn't.

Scooting forward, Pen cupped my face before she leaned in and kissed me. "I do love you, Walker, but I don't want you to do anything you'll regret later. This is something you really need to think about."

"The only thing I know is I will regret it for the rest of my life if I let the opportunity of having you forever slip by. Everything else, we can figure out when the time comes. I want you, Penelope Rose. Today, forever, always."

"Holy fucking shit, I think I have hearts in my eyes after hearing that speech."

"I know," Cross said. "This makes me kind of wish I had a girl."

"Nah," Kenton said. "You don't want to be tied down to one woman. Think of all the pussy we've been getting because Walker casts aside any woman who looks at him."

I nodded toward them. "Who needs kids when we have them?"

"Certainly not me." Pushing forward, Pen rested her forehead to mine. Her face lit up as she asked. "Are we really going to do this?"

"Hell, yes, we are. Now we just need to figure out how to get married here, and fast."

CHAPTER TWENTY-TWO

pen

LAUGHING, we stumbled out of our room, drunk on love and with very little sleep. For the last two weeks, Walker had been ravenous for me. He couldn't get enough, not that I was complaining. I loved every second, every touch, and every bliss-filled moment with him.

"Wow," came Greer's voice from down the hall. "You're not even trying to hide it now, are you? I can't believe you're being so stupid with your lives."

Walker growled from beside me as he took a step forward, ready to lunge at his bandmate. If we didn't have back-to-back shows the next two days, I probably would have let him. Instead, I tried to soothe the raging beast that wanted to tear Greer apart.

Running my hand up his arm, I grabbed Walker by the

bicep and tried to pull him down the hall. "Don't listen to him. He doesn't know what he's talking about."

"He sure as hell doesn't. If he knows what's good for him, he'll keep his fucking mouth shut." He moved like he was going to attack Greer, but it was all for show. His body was humming as he grabbed my hand and walked quickly down the hall toward the elevator. He was walking so fast; I had to jog to keep up with him.

"Hey," I cupped the side of his face with my hand after we stepped inside. "Greer was just being... Greer. You know he's an asshole even on his best days."

Looking down at me, his dark eyes softened, and he nodded. "I know, but I don't like the way he talks to you. He was fully on board with you being our manager, and now... I don't know. Maybe he's always sensed my attraction to you, and he feels the same." Walker shrugged. The space between his brows puckered.

"Well, it doesn't matter if he was ever interested in me because the feeling is not mutual." I ran my hands up his chest and around his neck. I wanted to kiss away the frustration that lined his face, but the moment I started to tug him down to me, the doors dinged open, and we were back in the real world.

Putting a couple of feet between us, we walked out to find Kenton and Cross talking to a few women in the lobby. If those two weren't careful, they were going to get an

STD or worse. Luckily for them, I kept them fully stocked with condoms.

"Are you two coming to eat with us, or did you make other plans?" Walker asked as we walked toward the entrance.

While I loved both Cross and Kenton, I hoped they said no. It was rare for me and Walker to get any alone time outside of our room. It would be nice to have dinner with only him.

They looked the girls up and down and then said their goodbyes, jogging to catch up to us.

The moment we set foot outside, Walker leaned down, placed his hands on his knees, closed his eyes, and took in a deep breath.

"What's eating you?" Cross asked, looking between Walker and me. "Is there already trouble in paradise?"

Walker stood, grabbed my hand, and started down the sidewalk without looking back. I gave them a tight smile over my shoulder. It didn't take but a second for Kenton and Cross to be on either side of me.

"Greer caught us coming out of my room." They both frowned, looking toward Walker, instantly understanding why he was in the mood he was. "Yeah, it didn't go the best, and he made it seem like he'd known about us."

"Why do you say that?" Cross asked.

"Because he said something like we weren't even trying to hide it anymore."

"Well," Kenton drew out. "You're not as careful as you could be."

"He hasn't said anything to us," Cross added. "Do you think he'll go to Cristiano with the news?"

I started to gnaw on my bottom lip at the thought. We should have been more careful. It would kill me to be fired and for Crimson Heat to get another manager.

Cross tried to put his arm around my shoulders, but Walker wasn't having it. He stopped dead in his tracks as if he could sense Cross's intentions and glared at him.

"We won't let anything happen to you," Walker vowed, leaning down until our eyes met. "Do you hear me?"

"Yeah, I know you won't. I can still worry about, it though."

Sometimes it scared me with how much conviction he had in his words. Like tonight. I couldn't let my fuckups cost him what he loved most.

"I thought we were going to order an Uber to take us to that restaurant?" Kenton asked.

Shit, I'd totally forgotten about the Uber I'd ordered. Pulling out my phone, it looked like our driver hadn't made it to the hotel yet. "We need to head back to the hotel where he's supposed to pick us up."

We walked single file down the sidewalk back to our

hotel to wait for our ride. I was happy Greer had previously said he was going to eat with some of the crew; otherwise, our dinner would have been more than awkward. Ever since Greer left our lunch in Greece, he'd been spending more and more time away from us, which was fine by me.

Thirty minutes later, we were being seated in a small restaurant up on North Bondi hill overlooking the ocean. I already felt more relaxed just seeing the ocean out the windows.

"Do you think we could go surfing tomorrow?" Kenton asked as he watched a bunch of surfers packing up their gear into their trucks.

He knew the answer to his question before he asked. "The answer to that would be a resounding no. It's in your contract that you can't do anything that would get you hurt, and surfing is one of those things."

"What if I promised not to get hurt," he looked at me, his big brown eyes giving me his best puppy dog eyes.

"I wish I could, but not unless you can convince Cristiano to give you a waiver that you'll pay back all the money the tour would lose if you got hurt."

"Fuck that," Kenton huffed out.

That's what I thought.

I'd barely picked up my menu to decide what I was having when my phone rang. Greer's name lit up the screen, and a pit of doom settled in my stomach. I wasn't sure why he was calling me, but whatever it was couldn't be good. I showed Walker my phone before I took the call.

"Hello?" I asked innocently—like he hadn't just seen Walker and me together only an hour ago.

"Pen?" He was quiet for a long moment before he cleared his throat. "Um, I need your help." The words sounded strangled on his tongue. It was probably difficult for him to ask for my help, and as much as I didn't want to help him. It was my job.

"Okay, where are you?" I pushed up from the table.

"I'm not sure. I'll figure out how to send you my location from my phone." Before I could say anything else, Greer hung up the phone.

I wasn't sure how easily I'd be able to figure out his location from what he sent me. I didn't have people sending me their locations often, but I would find him and then kick his ass.

Walker stood up, ready to follow me to the end of the Earth if I asked it of him. "What's up?"

"He's in trouble and asked for my help. You guys enjoy dinner, and I'll see you at the hotel." I turned to Kenton and gave him my best don't do anything stupid stare. "Don't go surfing."

He held his hands up. "I won't. You've got enough problems."

"Thanks." I gave him a grateful smile. Walker moved around the table and grabbed my hip. Looking up at him, I took in his concerned face. "What are you doing?"

"I'm going with you." He said it so matter of factly like I should have known what he planned to do.

Putting my hands on his chest, I tried to push him toward the seat he had vacated. I wasn't sure what I was thinking because if Walker didn't want to move, he wouldn't, and he wasn't on board with me going alone. "That's sweet of you, but I'm a big girl. You need to stay here. I don't know what kind of trouble Greer's in, but I think if he sees the two of us together, it will only cause more problems."

"I hate that you're right," he grumbled. His eyes scanned the room before he dipped down and planted a kiss on me that had me even more pissed off that I had to leave his side instead of dragging him to the nearest dark alley. He grinned down at me wickedly, letting me know he knew exactly how he'd left me. "If you need me, call me."

All I could do was nod. I knew I'd sound all breathy and wanton if a single word came out of my mouth.

Leaving the restaurant, I looked back and saw all the guys watching me through the windows. I gave them a sad little wave because I'd rather be sitting in there with them than bailing Greer out of whatever trouble he got himself in. I wasn't sure what kind of trouble he thought I could get him out of. I was a band manager, not a lawyer, and if I had to involve Titan's lawyers, it was not going to be good for him or me.

Luckily the location sharing worked and gave me an address. It should at least get me in the general direction of where he was. Once my Uber arrived to pick me up, I tried texting Greer to make sure he hadn't left but got no response. If this was some joke, if he was trying to play me, I was going to rip his balls off. I had a feeling, though, it hurt him just as much to ask for my help as it did for me to come to his rescue.

We pulled up to a bar that wasn't far from the hotel. At least it wouldn't take me long to get him back to the hotel once this was all settled.

I sent off a text to Walker letting him know where I was as I stepped into the bar. It didn't take me long to find Greer. He was yelling at two policemen who looked like they were on the verge of tasing him if they did that sort of thing in Australia.

The moment Greer saw me, he sagged against the officer's hold.

"Thank fuck you're here, Pen," he sighed out. "You've got to help me."

I gave my best smile as I looked at the policemen before turning to Greer. "What happened? Are you being arrested?"

"I hope not, but they sure as shit want to. I didn't know I was doing anything wrong. Those fuckers over there bet me a hundred bucks that I wouldn't run around the bar with a Batman mask on. One second, I'm laughing at my win, and the next, I've got these two on me saying they're going to take me to jail."

Cocking my head to the side, I tried to digest the story Greer just told me. "Did you only have the mask on?" The only reason I could come up with why they wanted to arrest him was Greer had on streaking across the bar.

"Yes, he only had on the mask. If he had on the entire costume, he'd be in the back of our squad car already," a tall, blond, surfer-looking officer answered.

"Was he naked while he ran around the bar?"

"What?" Greer shouted. "Of course not. I had on my clothes *and* the mask. Even I'm not drunk enough to go streaking in a foreign bar.

"Okay, let me get this straight. You want to arrest him for wearing a Batman mask?" This made absolutely no sense.

"Correct," the other officer with a squat build and a buzz cut answered. "It's illegal to wear a Batman costume."

What kind of fucked up shit was this?

I wanted to laugh, and later I would, but for now I needed to fix this.

Greer slurred something that I was sure wasn't nice, but luckily it was so incoherent no one understood him.

"I'm sorry. I doubt if my *friend* here knew it was illegal; otherwise, he wouldn't have put the mask on. In the United States, we love Batman, and there are tens of thousands who dress up like him every year for Halloween, if not more." Putting my hands on my hips, I looked around the room, trying to find who had bet Greer to put the mask on. Whoever it was, was obviously trying to get him in trouble. He was probably being an asshole, and they were trying to get rid of him.

I turned back to the officers. "If I offer to take him back to his hotel room, will you please let him go? Greer had no idea what he agreed to was illegal."

The two policemen looked at each other, having a silent conversation. If this didn't work, I wasn't sure how I'd get Greer out of this mess.

"If you promise to take him to his hotel, and he'll never come back to this bar or wear a Batman costume again."

I wanted to ask if that applied only in Australia or if it included the entire planet Earth because this was ridiculous. As much as I disliked Greer, he didn't deserve to be arrested over something so stupid.

"I promise. I'll take him there myself and make sure he doesn't come back here."

The officer's hold on Greer loosened before he let go.

"I hope you learned your lesson. You won't always have a pretty lady to get you out of trouble."

Greer's lip curled, and I knew something nasty was getting ready to come out. Clamping my hand over his mouth, I pulled him out of the bar and out onto the sidewalk.

I whirled around on him. "What were you doing? I thought you didn't want to go to jail."

"Not for something stupid like wearing a mask," he sneered and tried to pull his hand out of mine. I didn't let go, though. There was no way in hell I was going to let him get into more trouble.

"Let go," he demanded.

"No. Not until you're in your room. Then we're going to order us dinner because I'm starving, and you need to sober up. Then you're going to tell me what your problem is with me."

Greer yanked on my hand, causing me to become unbalanced and fall. I caught myself on my hands and knees. The instant I hit the pavement, I knew both would come up bloody. I stayed down, looking up at Greer, who was now circling me on the sidewalk.

Looking up at the sky, Greer yelled. The words dripped with so much pain that I felt it deep in my gut. "You want to know what my problem is with you? With the world?"

"Yes," I whispered to him as I stood up and moved in front of him.

"My problem is I want the one person I can never have," he cried out.

"Greer," I put my hand out to comfort him, but he swatted it away.

"It's not you, woman," he said the last word with so much venom I took a step back.

"I want Walker. He's who I want and will never have," he confessed, a lone tear streaming down his face.

Walker, Cross, and Kenton stepped out of the shadows as if on cue, all eyes on us. When had they gotten here? "Well, that explains a lot."

CHAPTER TWENTY-THREE

walker

LOOKING UP FROM MY PHONE, I spotted Greer looking over at me, but the second our eyes met, he turned his head to look away. It had been two weeks of this awkward dance. He wouldn't talk to me or anyone else on the bus. The only people he talked to were the crew members.

I felt bad. Unrequited love, lust, like, or whatever the hell he felt for me was a bitch. I couldn't do anything about it, though, and unfortunately for Greer, those feelings would never be reciprocated.

Pen felt awful and had been keeping too much space between us when Greer was around, which felt constant. I thought with all of the guys knowing, we wouldn't have to hide, but now it felt like we were hiding more than ever.

Pen came bounding into the room. There was a

bounce in her step and a wide smile. You could feel the happiness coming off of her in waves.

"I've got amazing news," she squealed. Picking up my hand, she held it to her chest as she faced the others. "I just got off the phone with Cristiano."

"Is that why you're so happy? Not that I blame you," Cross joked.

"No, silly," she swatted at him. "Twisted Youth just went gold," she called out the last word long and loud.

Cross leaned back against the wall across from me. His mouth hung open. "You've got to be fucking with us."

"I don't joke about business," Pen said before turning and jumping on me. I caught her effortlessly like I knew I would until the end of my days. She wrapped her body around mine, her fingers pulling on my hair until I was exactly where she wanted me, and then her lips were on mine.

With one hand under her ass, the other pulled her closer. The hard press of her mouth to mine had me wanting to forget the show we were supposed to perform in twenty minutes and take her back to the hotel where I could ravage her body all night long. That celebration would have to wait. Now it was time to revel in this moment with my brothers.

Breaking away, I pressed my forehead to Pen's before I placed one last kiss on her swollen lips and put her down.

She quickly moved out of the way as the guys and I converged in the middle of the room in a big hug where we all laughed, yelled, and maybe shed a tear or two. For once, even Greer was happy.

Cross was the first to step back from the group. He went directly to Pen and gave her a big bear hug, murmuring something to her that had her eyes misting up as she met my gaze. A watery smile graced her face as she rubbed his back.

"Let me get in on the love," Kenton broke away and hugged Pen and Cross from behind.

"Alright, while I love you all, you need to finish getting ready. Your set to be on stage in…" she looked down at her watch. "Ten minutes. You know the drill. Do what you need to do."

While Cross and Kenton disbanded from my woman, I prowled toward her and pulled her into my arms. "Does that include me?"

Tilting her head to the side, she shook her head with a touch of a smile. "Does what include you?"

Leaning down, I shadowed her body with mine and nipped at her earlobe. "Doing whatever I need to do before the show."

Penelope's arms wrapped around my waist and shoved her hands in my back pockets. "Is the intrigue already gone, and we've moved on to wham, bam, thank you, ma'am?"

Nuzzling her with my nose, I placed a kiss on the sensitive area right below her ear. "It most certainly isn't gone, but that doesn't mean we can't throw in a quickie every once in a while."

Her hands scratched up my back and along the nape of my neck. "You'll barely be getting started in ten minutes, but if you want me to blow you in the bathroom down the hall, I can do that."

The thought of Pen's sweet mouth on my cock nearly had me coming in my pants. I dragged her out of the room and to the bathroom, quickly locking the door. I'd barely turned around when my belt was unbuckled, and my zipper was down. Small, soft hands pulled me out of the confines of my briefs and started to slide up and down my length.

Getting down on her knees before me, Pen looked up at me from underneath her long lashes. Her whiskey-colored eyes locked with mine as she took my crown in her hot mouth and swirled her tongue around it.

"Fuck me," I groaned. "I love your mouth on me."

Pen hummed from her spot in front of me and slowly took my length until it hit the back of her throat, in and out in the slowest, most excruciating pleasure. She wasn't rushing it even though we only had a matter of minutes.

My sweet girl knew the power she had over me, and it wouldn't take me long as she expertly sucked me off.

Her hands moved to cup my ass, her nails digging into my flesh, and took me further down her throat than ever before. The feeling of her throat spasming around my length made me explode. Gripping her hair, I fucked her mouth until she tasted every last drop of me. Only then did I pull out and rim her pink, swollen lips with the tip of my cock.

"Fuck, baby, I'm not sure if I'm going to be able to perform. I think you sucked out all of my brain cells." I propped myself against the door, pulling her up as I did.

"I hope not because if you don't go out there and put on the best show of your life, then that's never happening again." She gave me a quick peck on the lips as if that was supposed to take the sting out of her words.

"Never as in before a show or never in my life?" I questioned as I tucked my slowly softening dick back into my pants. He wanted more, and so did I, but I knew that wasn't possible right now.

"That remains to be seen, so I suggest you get your ass out there and give me a show," she slapped my ass as I walked out of the bathroom.

Stopping just inside the little wall that separated the hall from the bathroom so no one could see us, I took her in my arms and just held her. We didn't get many moments like this since there were always people around. "I love you. You know that, right?"

Hugging me back, Pen rested her head on my chest and took a deep breath. I knew she was trying not to rush the moment even though I needed to be at the entrance of the stage. "I know you do, and I love you." She reclined back enough to see my face. "I'm so damn proud of you. Tonight, we'll celebrate right."

Pulling her hand up between us, I kissed the knuckles on both hands. "I happened to like our mini celebration."

"I bet you did. Now, go sing me a song," Pen pushed me out into the hall and then took her spot a couple of feet apart from me.

"All of my songs are for you, didn't you know?" Her lips looked so tempting. Would there ever be a time when I'd had enough of her?

She ran the back of her hand along my jaw before taking it away. Why was I always starved for her touch? We stopped a couple of feet away from where the band stood. "I do now. Love you, Walker."

"As I do you."

Was it wrong that I couldn't wait for this tour to be over, so I could spend every second of every day with her? This was my dream, and yet there was always this deep longing whenever Pen wasn't in my arms.

"Let's show them we're even better in person and hit platinum," Kenton said, walking backward onto the stage.

"Let's do this," Cross shouted as Kenton started pounding on his kit.

I walked out to a crowd of thousands of people screaming. I could even make a few calling our names. A smirk took over my face as I grabbed the microphone. "Good evening, London."

I STARED down at my phone in utter disbelief. I hadn't heard from my parents since the beginning of my junior year of college. I had messaged, letting them know we were going on tour, and never heard from them. They had firmly stated the last time I spoke with them that they wanted nothing to do with me if I pursued a career in music. I had wasted enough of their time and money.

Pen sat down next to me on the couch in our room. Her hand went to my knee as she leaned into me. "What's wrong?"

I flashed her my phone and the text message from my mom.

Mom: I heard one of your songs on the radio today.
I guess you really did make it.

Running her hand up and down my leg, Pen rested her head on my shoulder. "I'm sorry. I know how much it hurts not to have a parent's support, but at least she acknowledged what you've accomplished even if she could have been nicer about it."

I moved my thumb in order for her to read the rest of the message.

Mom: Now that you're famous, you can pay us back all that money we spent sending you to college.

Pen sat up with tears in her eyes. "Is she fucking serious right now?"

"Don't cry for me, my sweet Penny. I accepted long ago that my parents would never understand my love for music." I just never thought they'd be so callous as to ask for money the second they thought I had any money to my name.

"I can't help it. You hurt, I hurt. It's as simple as that." She moved then to straddle my thighs. Instinctively my hands settled on her hips, and my thumbs started to rub circles on the exposed skin between her jeans and shirt. "Do you think if you ignore her, she'll leave you alone?"

I shook my head because I had no idea. "I can't say. The people I grew up with... I don't know." I looked over her shoulder and out the window into the dark night. "My parents always told me that I could do or be anything when I grew up, and they'd be proud of me. I guess that was only if I was in a profession they approved of. From a young age, I was always singing, but something shifted when I was in high school, and I started my first band. All of a sudden, they were putting down my music and telling me I needed to get serious about school. It came out of nowhere. I mean, I was never awesome at school, but I wasn't bad. I passed my classes, but I was never an honor roll student."

"Aw, baby Walker, what I wouldn't give to see pictures of you as a baby and in high school." She kissed one eye and then the other. "I bet you were so cute and had all the girls hitting on you."

I wasn't falling for that trap. There was no way I was telling Pen about the girls I slept with in high school.

"I wasn't cute. In high school, I was lanky as I grew into this body."

"It's cute that you say that, but I know that isn't the truth. Maybe for a few months, but there's no way in hell you were some awkward, lanky kid all through high school."

"Oh, I wasn't awkward. I had game, no doubt about it," I said before thinking through what I was saying.

"That's what I thought. You don't have to hide yourself from me. I knew you weren't a virgin when we got together, just like you knew I wasn't. I'm not going to go out there and crack the skulls of every woman you slept with. Unless they hurt you." Her nostrils flared, and her cheeks got pink with anger. "Then they better watch out."

"You don't have to do that. No girl broke my heart. I was always very straightforward about what I wanted and expected. Now, you, on the other hand. I don't want to know how many guys you've been with or their names since I'm likely to kill any I come into contact with."

Pen rolled her lips and smiled. "You know I was having sex before you were born, so it's probably wise I don't tell you."

My hands gripped her hips, pulling her flush with me. "I don't care about those other men because I know I'm the last man you'll ever sleep with. It's not them who's got you in their bed every night."

Pulling on my bottom lip with her teeth, she then licked away the sting with her tongue. "Why is your jealousy so fucking hot?"

I opened my mouth to respond when my phone

notifications went off with another text. Moaning, I picked it up from where I'd dropped it on the couch to see another message from my mom.

Mom: Don't act like you didn't read my message. My phone shows it's been delivered and read. I expect payment when you're back in Willow Bay.

"I have a simple solution. I won't ever go back to Willow Bay," I growled out. What gave her the right to demand money from me? She had no idea how much I'd made.

"I hate to say this, but you promised your friend Merrick you'd go to his graduation." She was right; I had, and my mom would probably be stalking the graduation ceremony looking for me and her money. "You can't pay her. If you do it once, she'll keep coming back for more. Every time she hears one of your songs, she'll probably see dollar signs. I'll call the lawyers and see what they have to say."

Pen started to get off my lap, but I needed her. My mom and the lawyers could wait. "Let's forget about them until tomorrow. We're supposed to be celebrating." My hand slipped under her shirt and ran up the side of her ribs to cup her full breast. "Remember how my album went gold?"

Her body arched into my touch. "As if I could ever forget," she moaned, picking up my other hand and placing it over her other breast. "Touch me like you mean it."

Flipping Pen onto her back, I slipped off her shoes and leisurely started to divest her of her clothes. Pen squirmed and tried to hurry me, but I wanted to take my time and worship her the way she deserved. Sitting back on the couch, I pulled her feet onto my lap and started massaging them.

"What are you doing?" She laughed and then moaned when I hit a sore spot.

"I'm giving you a massage, and going by the way you're pushing your foot further into my hand, I think you want it." I dug my thumb into the pad of her foot.

"I will always take a massage, but I'm not used to getting one naked." She wiggled her other foot for it to get the same attention I was giving the other.

"I sure as hell hope no one is giving you naked foot massages." I switched feet and started on the other.

"You know what would make this better?" She groaned, her eyes falling closed.

Was she going to orgasm over a foot massage?

"No, what's that?" My hands moved up to start massaging her calf.

"If you were naked. I'm not sure why you have your clothes on." Pen stuck out her bottom lip in a fake pout.

"Because if my clothes were off right now, you wouldn't be getting this massage. I like being able to look at you." All her creamy flesh laid out just for me, her lush curves on display. The way her breathing picked up as I took her in.

"I like looking at you too. Your body is perfection personified."

"Do you only like me for my body?" I said in a joking matter.

The soft look on Pen's face disappeared completely. "Not even for a second. Yes, it's a perk, but I love you for you. I like how with others, you're quiet and kind of broody, but with me, you've never been anything but sweet. You're the total package, inside and out."

"That's enough massaging." I moved off the couch and onto my knees. Splaying Pen's legs wide, I licked up the inside of her thigh and straight to her core. Swirling my tongue around her nub, I ran my tongue through her slick folds, around her puckered hole, and back up again. I would never get tired of the taste of her. If I could mainline Pen's pussy I would.

"Stop torturing me and take off your clothes." Her hips bucked up as I sucked on her lips. "I need to feel you inside of me."

Standing, I started to unbuckle my belt and watched as Pen's chest started rising faster, her eyes darkening. "I want to watch you touch yourself like the first night we spent together."

One hand went to her chest, where she started to massage her breasts and pluck on her nipples. Her other hand slowly descended down her toned stomach to her slick pussy. Two fingers slid inside as the palm of her hand ground on her clit.

Arching in pleasure, Pen bit her bottom lip. "This better end with your big cock inside of me."

"Don't you worry about that. I promise I'm going to fuck you all night long, but for now, keep doing what you're doing."

"You sure do know how to sweet talk a girl." Her eyes darkened as fingers moved faster, pumping in and out, all the while watching me take off my clothes. I might have slowed down to prolong us watching each other.

The second my clothes hit the floor, Pen moved up to her knees and ran her slick fingers over my lips. I lapped at her finger and sucked off her taste.

"Turn around with your front to the back of the couch," I ordered. Kneeling on the couch behind her, I grabbed her ass and gave it a rough squeeze. From behind, I ran my length through her slick folds and lined myself up at her entrance. "Put your hands behind your back," I demanded and cuffed both of her hands with my free hand. Easing myself inside until I was fully submerged in Pen's heat, I let out a sigh. This was my home. Pen was my home. My heart. My forever.

Pen reared back, spurring me to move. Pulling back, I slammed into her, making us both moan. The way her walls fluttered around me, I knew I wasn't going to last long. I was too ramped up after wanting to be inside her for hours. With each thrust, I slapped her ass and felt her pussy clench around me, sucking me further inside. Her walls hugged my cock as if it was unwilling to let go until I exploded deep inside of her. Letting go of her hands, I pressed my front to her back and kissed up the nape of her neck.

Slipping out of her hot core, I picked her up and cradled Pen in my arms. She gave me a lazy smile as her head lulled against my chest. "What do you say we take a shower or maybe take advantage of that big bathtub in there?"

"Oh, a hot bath sounds nice." Her hand ran up my chest and around my neck. "Are you getting in with me?"

"And miss the opportunity to feel you all wet while riding my cock? Not a chance in hell." I pulled one of the robes off of the bathroom door and set it down on the counter before sitting Pen on top of it.

I turned on the water and looked around the bathroom

for some bubble bath. I looked high and low but found none.

"What are you looking for?"

"Bubble bath. I don't know why they don't have any if they're going to have this big tub." I opened a bottle of shampoo and poured some out under the spray. "This will have to do."

Hopping off the counter, Pen walked over to me like a dream and hugged me with her head on my chest. "We could call down to the front desk for some."

"I'm not waiting for them. I want to see you all suds up now.

"It's like you're reading my mind," she said as she stepped inside the tub and sunk into the water.

Slipping inside, I washed Pen from head to foot before I sat her on my lap and let her ride me with abandon. By the time we left the tub, half the water had been splashed out onto the floor.

We fell asleep sweaty and wrapped around each other after a perfect night of celebrating.

CHAPTER TWENTY-FOUR

pen

I TRIED to swallow the lump in my throat, but the pressure only increased. Any minute now, I wouldn't be able to breathe.

Was my world about to come crumbling down around me?

Cross walked into my office at my condo and then promptly stopped. "Shit, Pen, are you pregnant?"

My head whipped up. "What? No," I laughed bitterly. "Why would you ask me that?"

"Because you look sick."

Did I? I wouldn't doubt it after the message I just received. I couldn't let Cristiano see me looking any worse for wear. We'd been back for all of one day when I was summoned, although I was supposed to have a week off before we decided what was next for Crimson Heat.

Walker took a step into the room and then another

before he was right by my side. Kneeling down beside me, he asked. "What's wrong?"

"Cristiano," was all I managed to say. I handed my phone to Walker and let him see the message I received only twenty minutes ago. I'd been frozen until Walker appeared.

"What do you think it's about?"

"I don't know. He's never been to my house, and for him to demand to see me here… it can't be good." My hands shook as I asked. "Do you think he knows?"

"Maybe, but it will be okay. I promise."

"I hope you're right. What's Cross doing here? Maybe the two of you should leave before Cristiano gets here," I rambled nervously.

"I'm not leaving you here to deal with all of this by yourself if it's what we think it is. I pursued you, and I wouldn't leave you alone."

"I am perfectly capable of handling myself. I didn't have to give in to you." I wilted against his strong frame.

"I beg to differ," he smirked cockily at me. "I'm pretty hard to resist."

"And when you talk like that, I wonder how I ever gave you the time of day." I rolled my eyes at him while also smiling at him. The happiness drained from me the second my phone went off, letting me know someone was downstairs.

Walker gripped my hands. "Alright, let's take a deep breath, and everything will be fine."

"I'll answer the door while you get yourself together." Cross backed out of the room. I hadn't noticed when he walked into the room. "You might want to put on your jewelry before he gets up here."

I shuffled out of the room and into my bedroom, where I put on my watch, earrings, and rings along with a swipe of lip gloss. I wanted to look as put together as possible. There was no way I was going to let Cristiano see he'd unnerved me by his dropping by spur-of-the-moment.

"Why am I not surprised you two are here?" I heard Cristiano sneer from the other room. I walked into the room to see Cristiano circling Cross and Walker. "Is she doing the both of you or the whole band?"

"You son of a bitch." Walker cocked back his fist and lunged for Cristiano. I couldn't let him hit Cristiano. If he did, Walker's career would be over, and I wouldn't let that happen over a few words out of Cristiano's mouth.

Grabbing onto his arm, he swung with the power of a freight train. The punch missed my boss, but the momentum kept going, throwing me into the coffee table. My side hit, and I knew I'd have a nasty bruise, but I wasn't going to show that I was in pain. Not with Cristiano looking down at me with distaste.

"Fuck, Pen," Walker shouted, running to me. He

picked me up in his arms and sat us down on the couch with me on his lap as he ran his hands over my body.

"You can put me down. I'm fine. I just hit my side." I jerked as his hand found a tender spot.

"You're not fine. God, I'm so sorry. I wanted to be here to protect you, and all I've done is hurt you myself."

"I'll be fine." I pushed his hands away and sat next to him on the couch. "Why are you here, Cristiano?" I wanted to get down to business and get this over with.

"Because I wanted to see all of this in person. I didn't believe it when I heard you were stupid enough to be sleeping with one of your clients. Do you know how bad this will make Titan Records look? For fuck's sake, Pen, you could be his mother." The way he looked at me with pure disgust made my stomach roil.

At the same time, both Walker and Cross started to go for Cristiano. "Don't," I yelled, moving to get between them and my ugly boss.

Lucky for me, this time, they heard me. Cross moved to sit in the chair beside me, and Walker took me back to the couch, the whole time glaring at Cristiano. "Don't talk to her like that. I love this woman, and what we have is the best thing that's ever happened to me, even over you signing our band."

"Wow, kid, her pussy's got you brainwashed. What Pen did was mess with your little young head, or should I say your other head," he laughed the ugliest laugh. I cringed back from the viciousness of his words, wanting to be nowhere near it. "We'll get you a new manager that won't take advantage of you."

"You shut your mouth," Walker gritted out. "If anyone took advantage of anyone, it was me."

"Oh, please, kid, you don't know what you're talking about," Cristiano laughed. He looked over at me and ground his molars together. "You're never going to work in this industry again."

Walker laughed, a cruel sound I'd never heard from him before. "You can't do that. See, it states in our contract that Pen is to be our manager. If you fire her, you lose us."

"Do you seriously think I care if I lose you? You're one in a million, kid. Did you know Ms. Rose's contract says she will not have any sexual relations with her clients?"

"It's Mrs. Pierce, or did you miss that part?" Walker lifted my left hand to show off the ring that sat on my finger.

Cristiano furrowed his dark brow. "What are you talking about? Her name is Pen Rose."

Taking Walker's left hand in mine, I rubbed my thumb over his black wedding band. "We got married in Greece." I tilted my head to the side. "Did your source tell you that?"

"No, he didn't," Cristiano stuttered out.

.   .   .

"I'm sorry to interrupt." *Breaking away from Walker, we looked over to find a sweet old woman standing at the end of our table. She smiled kindly as we looked at her. "I couldn't help but overhear you want to get married here in Oia but don't have a lot of time."*

"We only have tonight. We leave tomorrow and will be on the road for the next two months. Do you know of a place we can get married on such short notice?"

Clasping her withered hands together, the old woman smiled. "I think I do as long as you have your passports and an Apostilled birth certificate."

"Yes, we have all of those things. In fact, I have them in my purse."

"What the hell are you doing carrying all of that?" Kenton laughed.

"Because I never know when we'll need it and today is my lucky day that I carry all of our paperwork in my purse." I held up my giant purse that could take a person out if they were ever hit with it.

"Perfect. My daughter works at the town hall, and I bet I can get her to push the paperwork through for you once she sees how in love the two of you are. If you could come with me, we can get the paperwork done, and it would be my honor to officiate the wedding at any location you'd like."

We hit the jackpot with this woman overhearing us.

"Oh, yes, could we get married on the hill overlooking the Aegean Sea?" I gushed, and I never gushed. Was I really doing this?

"Anything you want, my dear. Why don't we see if we can get the paperwork to go through, and then if you want to do some shopping for some wedding attire or rings, you can do that." She looked down at her watch and smiled. "You have a little over three hours until sunset, so we should get moving."

I jumped up and gave the woman a hug. "You have no idea how much this means to us. Thank you… What's your name?"

The old woman patted me on the back and smiled over at Walker. I wasn't sure what we would have done without her. The look Walker was giving me seemed as if he was afraid if I had a chance to think too long about marrying him, I might back out after hearing all of Cross and Kenton's questions. It didn't matter, though, because I knew deep down in my soul we were perfect for one another.

She patted my cheek and smiled. "My name is Sofia."

"That's such a beautiful name. I'm Penelope, and this is my… fiancé, Walker."

"It's very nice to meet you both." Walker stood and shook her delicate hand. Before he could pull back, she leaned and whispered, "I hope you get her one hell of a ring because you've got a priceless gem on your hands."

"I will," he promised. Leaning in further, he asked, "Can you tell me where I can find something like that here?"

"Of course, dear," Sophia turned and clapped her hands. "Let's get on our way. We've got much to plan."

Unwilling to waste another moment, I pulled out a wad of cash and threw it down on the table. I hadn't even thought about paying for the food we hadn't eaten. "Can you get the rest boxed up and meet us when you're done?" I asked the guys.

Kenton looked down at all the food. "If we don't eat it all."

"You can't have me passing out on my wedding day, now, can you?"

"I guess we can't. Fine," he sighed like it was going to hurt him not to eat it all. Seriously, we had enough food for ten, and there were only four of us now. Surely there could be some left over for us to eat before we got married.

I couldn't believe it. With what felt like every blink I took for the day, something changed, and in a few short hours, I would be married.

I linked my hand with Walker's and gave it a squeeze as we followed Sofia out of the restaurant. "I hope you're ready for this."

Brushing his lips to mine, he pulled back and vowed. "More than anything. Now let's go make this official," he said as he slapped my ass.

CROSS STEPPED in front of us with his arms over his chest. "You know what? I don't think we need you. Pen, start your own record label, and we'll be the first to sign."

"Let's not be hasty," Cristiano backtracked.

"Maybe you shouldn't have come in here throwing out all that trash talk. Pen has worked her ass off for us, and I believe if it wasn't for her pushing every step of the way, we wouldn't be here. And the thing is, I think she can do that for every band that needs someone like her. What do you say, Pen? Do you want to start your own label with us? I'll happily chip in all of my money to help you get started. I'm sure Kenton would as well."

Walker's grip on my hand tightened, making me look at him. This was all too much. Never in a thousand years did I think today would turn out this way, nor had I ever thought of creating my own label, but now that it had been put out there in the world, I could see it.

"I'm in, and I'll be right by your side through the whole thing. We can do this," he nodded like all of this made sense.

"I… I don't know. One second I'm getting fired, and the next, you guys are telling me I should create a label?" I looked down at my bare feet and wiggled my toes. "I'm a little overwhelmed here."

"Well, I'll make the choice for you. You're fired. I don't know how you got this boy to marry you, and it probably isn't even legal. Titan Records can't get behind employees who take advantage of their clients. You're fired, Ms. Rose or *Mrs. Pierce,* whatever your name is."

My world started to sink below me. This wasn't how it was supposed to happen. We were supposed to show we were married, and then everything would be fine. How could I be so stupid?

"Don't bother coming into the office to clear out your things. I'll have them ship your stuff to you." Cristiano pushed by us, and all I could do was watch him go.

"Baby," Walker whispered in my ear from behind. When had his arms enveloped me? "It's going to be okay." Turning in his arms, I shook my head. Lifting one hand, he cupped the side of my face. His thumb ghosted over my cheek. I leaned into his touch, never wanting it to leave. With his simple touch, I felt safe. "We can do this. Even if you don't want to start your own label, we don't need Titan Records. We can produce our own music. You have the knowledge, and we have the talent."

I leaned into his body, clutching his shirt with my hands. "I can't make that decision today, and you shouldn't either."

"I think you two should be alone, so I'm going to head out. Whatever you decide, I'll support you."

"Thanks, man," Walker looked over my shoulder with an uptick of his lips. "I'll text you later, and we'll figure this all out."

"I'll see you later, Pen." Cross's hand came down on my shoulder and gave me a small squeeze.

"Okay, thank you for being here." I couldn't take my

eyes off Walker. I knew once I did, everything would come crumbling down.

"Of course," he answered back before I heard the door click shut.

With knitted brows, Walker pulled me to him. Our bodies pressed together, the rapid beating of his heart let me know my husband wasn't as serene as he was pretending.

"What's going on with you?" He started to shake his head in denial, but I wasn't having any of that. I needed him to say what he was feeling. "Tell me."

Closing the windows to his soul, he took in a deep breath before he let it out and spoke with a tortured voice. "Do you regret marrying me?"

I gasped and would have staggered back if he wasn't holding onto me. "What are you talking about? Look at me," I demanded.

Slowly, his eyes opened, and I could see the torment swirling in their depths. His Adam's apple bobbed as he swallowed hard. "Now that you got fired from your dream job, there's no reason to be married to me."

I swore I must have still been in shock because I wasn't sure how I didn't slap some sensed into him right then. How could he ever think that? "How about the reason I married you is because I love you? I would never have married you to keep my job. Did we get married on a fabulous spur-of-the-moment decision? Yes, but I wouldn't change it for anything. Is the reason you're asking because you regret what I might cost you?"

Walker let out a booming laugh, although I didn't find anything funny about what we were talking about. "There's no way in hell you're getting rid of me. Not now, after what you just said. You, Penelope Pierce, are stuck with me until the end of time." Lacing the fingers of our left hands together, Walker placed them over his heart. "Now that the news is out, I don't want us to ever take off our rings. I want to show the world that I'm taken by you."

Pressing my forehead to our joined hands, I took in his words and how they filled my chest with warmth. "Sometimes, the words you speak to me sound like a love song." Moving to rest my chin on our hands, I gazed up at him, feeling butterflies take off deep in my belly. "I love how fiercely you love me."

Nudging my chin with our hands, Walker lifted it as he simultaneously dipped down until our lips were only a breath apart. "Let me show you how I love you. Let me worship you, and tomorrow we'll figure out what our future holds together."

CHAPTER TWENTY-FIVE

walker

"WHERE ARE WE GOING AGAIN?" Greer grumbled from the backseat.

"How many times do we have to tell you?" Kenton huffed from beside him. Our eyes met in the rearview mirror, and he rolled his eyes. "It's a party slash photoshoot at Pen's friend's house. She came to visit Pen when we were in Amsterdam."

"Whatever. How long is this going to take? I've got better things to do."

"What, like finally getting the stick out of your ass?" Cross asked, snickering from beside me.

"Once we get the shots for the band, you can leave at any time," I gritted out.

It had been almost two weeks since Cristiano showed up and fired Pen. The only person that any of us could figure out would tell Cristiano about Pen and me was Greer. The thought that he'd betrayed us after Pen got him out of being arrested made my blood boil. Today was the first day any of us would be around him, and I wasn't sure how it was going to go down. Would he confess? Would we kick him out of the band? Or would he leave once he found out the news of Pen and me being married? We had no idea. All I knew was today was going to be an interesting day.

Because of traffic, we pulled up to the house almost an hour later. Pen's car was in the driveway of the house next door where her best friend Stella lived. Before we could get out of the car, Stella and her boyfriend, Remy, came out of the house.

Stella ran up to me and instantly wrapped her arms around my waist. I patted her back awkwardly. While I'd been around Pen when she talked to Stella, I'd only been around her twice before today. Plus, I wasn't a touchy-feely person. Unless it was Pen, then I couldn't stop touching her. "It's so good to see you," she said loud enough for everyone to hear and then spoke quietly enough for me. "She looks beautiful. Today is going to be epic."

I started to walk toward the house when Stella caught me. "She's in the back waiting for you."

"Thanks," I said gruffly. I couldn't wait to see Pen. She was gone by the time I woke up today in preparation for what was about to go down, and I knew she was going to blow my socks off when I saw her.

"Everyone," Stella announced as we moved around the car. "This is Remy. Remy, this is Walker," she swept her hand in my direction, along with the rest of the band. Stella grimaced. "I'm sorry, I know names, but I'm not sure if I know exactly who they belong to."

The guys all introduced themselves, with Greer giving me a dirty look. "Of course, she knows who you are."

I paid him no mind. I wanted to get inside and see Pen, but that didn't go according to plan. The second we walked inside the beautiful house, we were stopped by Lexie.

"Hey, guys. We're all set up in the back. I thought we could eat lunch before we get started. My husband is out back grilling, so I hope you like burgers. If I know him, though, there's probably chicken as well. I've got to go grab my batteries, and then I'll be right out." Lexie swept out of the room, her blue hair bouncing as she went.

"This house is sweet," Kenton whistled.

He wasn't wrong. It was all modern, the back almost completely glass looking out at the Pacific. I wouldn't mind living here one day.

"Follow us," Stella and Remy moved past us and to the backyard.

I followed dutifully, wanting to see Pen. The second I

stepped outside, there she was in a long, light gold dress that showcased her curves with her hair up in an elegant twist.

I was standing in front of her within seconds. Taking her face in my hands as I stared down at her. "God, you're beautiful. I feel like we're getting married all over again." I looked down at the jeans and t-shirt I had on, then at the suit Pen had me bring that was draped over my arm. "Now the monkey suit makes sense."

Resting her hands on my waist, Pen grinned up at me. "You're going to need it when you win a Grammy."

"No, you've got to be kidding me, or are you serious?"

"Crimson Heat is going to the VMA's, and I know that's only the start. I don't know about you, but I've been busy all day, and I can't wait to eat before Lexie starts shooting you." She looked down at her dress. "I should probably get something to cover my dress, so when we get *our* pictures later, it won't have burger grease on it."

Gripping my shirt at the neck, I pulled it over my head and handed it to Penelope. "Put this on, and you can give it back to me when you finish eating."

Running her hands from my waistband up to my pecs, Pen licked her lips. "How am I supposed to eat with you sitting there without a shirt on?"

"Well, I don't know how I'm going to be able to eat knowing how you look under my t-shirt." Putting my arm around her waist, I walked us over to the grill, where everyone was standing around chatting.

Lexie took Pen in and laughed. "Well, that's new. Maybe we should have kept you out of your dress until after lunch?"

"Oh my God, Pen," Stella laughed. "All you need is a pair of combat boots, and you're rocker chic."

"I could get you a pair if you want to be in any pictures with the band," Lexie added.

Pen laughed, shaking her head, and making a tendril of hair fall out of her bun. She started to tuck it back behind her ear until I intercepted it and twisted it around my finger. "I won't be participating in that shoot. Only the one afterward." Tucking her hair behind her ear, I ran my knuckles along her jaw.

Crossing his arms over his chest, Greer's jaw ticked as he asked. "Why are you in that stupid dress?"

I wasn't sure why he was upset she was in a dress unless he'd figured it out. Even if I was crazy enough to let Pen go, there was never going to be anything between the two of us, so he needed to get over me and stop taking everything out on my wife.

The man at the grill, who I hadn't met yet, turned toward Greer with his blue eyes blazing. "We don't talk to ladies like that. Especially not in my house."

Greer looked him up and down, his nostrils flaring. "What are you going to do about?"

Lexie moved toward her husband with worried eyes and whispered his name.

Ryder pulled Lexie's body against his, never once taking his eyes off Greer. "I'll kick you out of my house for one. We opened our home up to you to do your shoot and to celebrate Pen and Walker. I won't tolerate disrespect."

Greer turned his gray eyes my way. A deep furrow between his brows. "What's he talking about?"

"Dimples, you let the cat out of the bag about the wedding," Lexie whispered, none too quietly.

"You're... getting married today?" Greer stuttered out, looking back and forth between Pen and me. I didn't like the way his eyes turned to slits as his gaze settled on her.

"Not today. We actually got married in Greece," I informed him.

"What?" He shouted and started to pace in front of us.

"Is he going to become a loose cannon?" Ryder asked his wife.

"I don't know, but I do not like this. This guy is an asshole and probably the one who ratted Pen and Walker out to her former boss." Again, Lexie spoke quietly, like she was trying to whisper, but loud enough for us all to hear.

Greer gripped the strands of his hair and pulled as he walked away from us before he sank down on a lounger.

Putting his elbows on his knees, he hung his head. "What the fuck is happening here?"

I moved to stand in front of him, ready to confront him about snitching to Cristiano about us.

Putting my hands behind my back so I didn't punch Greer, I asked, "Why don't you tell us what's going on? When did you tell Cristiano about Pen and me?"

"Why?" He opened and closed his mouth a few times. "How did you know?"

My hands balled into fists. "Maybe because Cross and Kenton have known since Greece and have been supportive of us, unlike you."

"Hey," Pen whispered from behind me as she placed her hand on my back. She ran it up and down, trying to help my rising temper, but nothing was going to help me. Greer had been like a brother to me, and he had betrayed me all because he thought he liked me. I wasn't sure if he was capable of liking anyone.

Greer shook his head and looked up at me with the saddest damn eyes that were filling up with tears. "Please tell me you didn't get married."

A low growl slipped from my lips as I stared down at him. "Why? I love Pen, and she loves me. It makes perfect sense for us to be married."

"I can't sit around and watch you two together. It's wrong," he gritted out between clenched teeth.

Widening my stance, I breathed in a harsh breath that did nothing to help my boiling blood. It wasn't until Pen laced her fingers with mine and pressed her forehead to my back that I stopped seeing red. "Look, I don't care that you're gay. I really don't, but there's never going to be anything between us. *Ever.* If you can't accept that I'm married to Pen, and she's not going anywhere, then you need to leave."

Greer stood abruptly and was instantly in my face. A snarl came out of him as he said, "She's using you. All she wants is your money."

I felt Pen break away from me before I heard her. She pushed between us and glared up at Greer. "Are you fucking serious right now? I want his money? No," she shook her head and laughed bitterly. "You need to open up your eyes before you're a distant memory. Stop pushing everyone away by being an asshole. I can't say I'm sorry Walker chose me over you because then I'd be without him, and without him, I'd be lost. I never expected any of this to happen. I just wanted to do my job, but day after day, Walker wormed his way into my heart." Her voice quieted, and if I wasn't standing at her back, I wouldn't have been able to see that she was shaking. "I understand why you think you love Walker. He's a great guy when he finally opens up and lets you in, and he's drop-dead gorgeous. But I believe if you really think about it, you'll realize it's just an infatuation. Someday you'll find your own dark Prince Charming."

"You don't know how I feel," Greer hissed back at her.

My arm went around her shoulders and pulled her back a step. "No, we don't know how you feel. All you've ever done was shut us out and be an asshole to us. We put up with it because you play damn good, but now…" I shook my head, hating what I was about to say. "I'm not sure…" My throat started to close up with emotion.

"Tell us something, Greer," Cross asked, moving to stand beside me. Kenton came to stand on my other side. "Did you tell Cristiano about them?"

"Yes, it was me," he growled out. "It should have been you. You should have said something the second you found out." He shook his head back and forth like a crazy person. "This never should have happened."

"It doesn't matter who it was. You would never have approved," Kenton started. "The thing you're not seeing is Walker isn't into guys, and he's never given any inclination he is. He's not going to switch teams for you."

"You don't know that," Greer shouted. He frantically eyed each of us like we were the bad guys.

"But I do," I spoke up. "Liking guys isn't in the cards for me. I'm sorry. I really am if this hurts you, but right now, you need to decide if you can accept that I love Pen and we're married. She is going to be with me every step of the way. I don't know how everyone else feels, but—"

"No, we agree with you," Kenton stepped in. I saw Cross nodding his head out of the corner of my eye. "We love Pen, not like you do Walk, but she's like a sister to us, and we want her with us, helping guide us through our journey."

Greer's face turned a deep shade of red as if he was holding his breath or about to explode at any second. "Are you seriously picking her over me?"

Cross stepped forward and put his hand on Greer's shoulder. "That's up to you. Can you accept Pen is always going to be around?"

Knocking Cross's hand off him, Greer stepped back. "I can't believe this. Haven't you ever heard of bros before hoes? No," he looked around the backyard, eyes darting every which way as if he was looking for an escape. "No, I don't accept this. I can't watch her ruin you."

Pen stiffened in my hold, and I knew I needed to end this. I didn't want Greer ruining today. We were supposed to be celebrating, and he was turning it into some soap opera drama I'd rather forget. "The only one who's being ruined is you. I'm sorry, Greer, but you're no longer in Crimson Heat."

"You're going to regret what you're doing here today when she leaves you high and dry—mark my words. You're never going to amount to anything," he spat out each word like a cobra strike.

I didn't let his words phase me. He was angry, and one day Greer would regret he couldn't accept what Pen and I had together.

"I hope I never see your ugly faces again." Greer didn't look back as he stalked through the house with Ryder following close behind. We all watched as he left and Ryder closed and locked the door behind him, and that chapter in all of our lives was closed for good. Greer wasn't a part of us any longer. I knew it was for the best, but it was still a hard pill to swallow.

Ryder walked back outside and back to the grill while everyone else stood staring at us.

Pen pulled away and headed toward the others. "I'm sorry that happened here. We should have confronted him before today." She sniffed. "I hate that I've wasted your time, Lexie."

"Oh, honey." Lexie went to Pen and put her hands on her shoulders. "You may not have thought it was going to go that way, but I knew it wasn't going to be good. I'll still take pictures of the rest of the band, and if or when you get another member, I'll do it again. But today is really about being with your friends and celebrating you and Walker. Let's eat, have some fun, get some pictures in, and at sunset, you can have your wedding day all over again."

Pen nodded, but it looked like a bobble. I knew everything was starting to sink in, and Pen would feel guilty when it all hit her. Stella seemed to realize the same thing. She was closer, and I let her have a quiet moment with her friend before I went to her.

With only a foot of space between us, Pen turned around as if she could feel me closing in. The tears in her eyes and the watery smile had me moving quicker to get to my girl. She was hurting, and it killed me to see.

Pen fell into my arms. Her body shook as she buried her face in the side of my neck.

"Baby, it's okay. We knew this was likely going to happen. How can we have Greer in our band when he went behind all of our backs?" I didn't think it would do him any good being around Pen and me, either.

"But how can you be Crimson Heat without a rhythm guitarist?" She muttered against my skin.

"We can find someone new. Someone better, who gets along with all of us and doesn't have the hots for me."

Pen laughed as I intended, her hot breath tickling my neck. "I'm sorry. I thought he might see reason, and because of me—"

"No, it's not because of you. It's all on him. No one blames you," I murmured into the top of her head.

"The band will be better without Greer in it," Cross said from somewhere behind us.

Leaning back with red-rimmed eyes, her chin wobbled. "First, you lose your label, and now Greer. I feel like I'm bad luck ever since you got back from tour."

Taking her face in my hands, I wiped my thumbs over the wetness on her cheeks. "Don't say that. You're my lucky Penny. Forever and always."

A throat cleared, causing us all to look toward the noise.

Ryder frowned and looked at Pen sympathetically. "I'm sorry to break up the moment, but lunch is ready." He looked to the table where the food sat waiting. "Is there anything I can do to make you feel better?"

"You can take off your shirt," Stella laughed. Her boyfriend narrowed his eyes at her. "What? You can't deny his hotness."

"Keep your shirt on, Ryder," Pen murmured as she walked over to the table where burgers, chicken, potato and every other kind of salad were laid out before us. Her voice was quiet as she took in all the food. "Thank you for providing lunch for us. We could have ordered and had it delivered or something."

Lexie hugged her husband's side. "Ryder loves to grill when he's home, and I'm not going to deny him the chance to grill."

"Thanks, baby." Ryder kissed her forehead. "Let's eat."

We all sat down to eat. Everyone was talking amongst

themselves, but Pen remained silent and still beside me. Sitting down with my burger, I turned to her. "Hey, it's going to be fine. I promise. In fact, I know we're going to be better than ever. Do you trust me?"

She nodded, her shoulders relaxing. "Of course, I do."

Putting my forehead to hers, I gave her a small kiss. "Good, now let's have fun with your friends and celebrate."

"You guys are so sweet," Stella cooed from across the table.

The doorbell went off, setting us all on alert. Our backs stiffened as we looked toward the front door, which you could see from outside.

Ryder stood, his jaw tense. "Any chance that's your friend?"

"Doubtful, but I'll go with you just in case. You shouldn't have to deal with him if it is."

Ryder nodded as I followed him inside the house. I stood back a few feet in case it wasn't Greer. Ryder pointed to a screen on the wall I hadn't noticed. To my shock and horror, my parents were standing on the other side of the door. "Do you know them?"

"Yeah," I croaked out and then had to clear my throat. "Those are my parents, but I didn't invite them here." In fact, I hadn't talked to either one of them since my mom called demanding money.

"I'll let you handle them and tell Pen for you," Ryder said, looking from the door to me.

Cracking open the door, I took in my parents for a moment. It had only been a little over a year since I last saw them. They looked older and angrier than I'd ever seen them before. I opened the door and asked. "What are you doing here?"

My father's dark eyes blazed with anger. "We gave you plenty of time to come see us, so we followed you."

"You followed me? This is a private residence, and you don't belong here."

My mom, whose hair used to be pure black, was now salt and pepper, looked down at the sidewalk she stood on. It was my dad who spoke, shocking me. "Listen, punk. We'll leave once you give us the money."

CHAPTER TWENTY-SIX

pen

JUST WHEN I thought the day couldn't get any worse, I heard Walker shout from outside Lexie and Ryder's house.

Ryder came outside. His usually happy face was anything but putting me on alert. "Hey, Pen, I think Walker's parents are here."

"What?" Cross jumped up from the table and looked at me. "Did you give them any money?"

"No, not a dime," I said as I rushed into the house.

"You need to leave," Walker growled as he attempted to keep his parents from coming inside.

"Why? Don't you want your fancy friends to know you owe us money?" An older man snapped. He was as tall as Walker and just as handsome, except his face was twisted in anger, and that anger was directed straight at his son.

Walker stepped back with his hands deep in his pockets. "Can you please explain to me how I owe you money?"

"We paid for your college. Two and a half years, and you threw it away for what?" His dad shrugged.

I moved in behind Walker, placing my hand on his back. His stiff posture relaxed more and more with each second I touched him. I only wished I could do more for him. Walker never talked about his parents. I think it hurt too much after they dismissed him for choosing to follow his dream.

"Well, I hate to inform you, but we're no longer with the label and lost a band member recently. I'm without a job, and Pen and me," Walker motioned for me to step forward from where I stood behind him. "This is my beautiful wife, Pen, we just bought a house, so I'm sorry to inform you, I have no money to give you."

We hadn't bought a house. The plan was to put our money into making their next album. That was, until a couple of labels called after hearing Crimson Heat was no longer with Titan Records, wanting to sign them. They were even supportive of our marriage. Now with Greer gone, we had no idea what would happen, but there was no way he was telling them that.

Once we got back from tour and after Cristiano fired me, Walker showed me the songs he'd written while we were apart. They were gut-wrenching and heartbreaking. Two things I knew that would sell. They were going to put Crimson Heat on the map as soon as they decided on the best label for them.

Walker's mom stepped forward. She was beautiful, which was to be expected since her son was such a knockout. Except now, her face was marred with a deep scowl, matching the expression of her husband. "You're an ungrateful little shit. Until you pay us back the money we paid for your college, I don't want to hear from you."

Someone behind me whispered a loud 'harsh,' but I wasn't sure who it was.

As a unit, they started to turn away until Walker spoke. "Don't you even want to meet my wife, your daughter-in-law?"

His dad turned and looked at us like he was looking through us, and my heart broke for Walker when he spoke his next words. "I don't know what you're talking about. How could I have a daughter-in-law when I don't have a son?"

Wrapping my sweet husband in a hug, all I wanted was to take away his pain. Walker's face was blank, but his charcoal eyes held all of his pain. I knew then that his parents had killed any kind of relationship they might have had.

I ran my hand up and down his back as I kept

muttering how sorry I was, but I knew my words couldn't soothe the burn they'd inflicted.

"I don't know what happened to them," he murmured robotically, looking at the now-closed door. "It's like something flipped inside them when I went to college. It was like once I was out of the house, they resented me. If money was a problem, I wish they would have said something. Even now, I don't know if they want the money because they hate me or if it's because they need it." Tipping his head down, all of his anguish was written in the stark features across his face.

Tears welled in my eyes as I looked up at him. "Maybe we should go and do this another day."

His fists tangled in the t-shirt I had on and pulled me closer as his turbulent eyes scanned my face. "There's no way in hell I'm going to let them ruin today. You, Stella, and Lexie spent a lot of time working on this, so we're going to go out there, eat, party, and have fun."

"I don't think anyone would fault us for rescheduling it for another day." Why was it that when you made plans, they always went to shit? It was one thing after another today.

"They wouldn't, but I might have arranged for us to have a little honeymoon after this. Somewhere it can finally be just the two of us."

"A honeymoon? I like the sound of that." Raising up

on my tiptoes, I brushed my lips over his and smiled against his mouth. "Where are we going?"

He hummed against my mouth, smiling. "I think I'll keep it a secret until we leave tonight."

"Tonight?" I jumped back. "Are you crazy? I have to pack, and to pack, I have to know where I'm going."

"I might have already packed for you," he smiled down at me with a wicked grin. "Your bag is in my car."

"I'm going to trust you to know what I need. It's not like I plan to be doing much other than you." Running my hand up his naked torso, I licked my lips as I took my husband in. I wasn't sure there would ever be a time when I got tired of looking at him or the way his body reacted when I touched him. My hand snaked around his neck to pull him closer to me. Now that I had kicked my heels off, Walker stood several inches over me just the way I liked it. There was something comforting about having a man who was big and strong. "Are you just going to stand there, or are you going to kiss me?"

"I happen to quite like the way you were looking at me," he smirked. "Do you want me to kiss you with an audience because I will if you want?"

"I don't care who's watching." And I didn't. I wouldn't care if he pulled me out on stage and ravaged me at this point. I wasn't going to hide how I felt from him in public ever again.

Dipping down, Walker swiped his tongue over the seam of my lips and delved in. I opened for him, meeting his tongue with mine. My eyes closed as we connected. After having to hide, there were times like these when all I wanted to do was kiss Walker and never stop. The kiss was over far too quickly for me, especially when I opened my eyes to see Walker smirking down at me. Gone was his earlier pain.

Taking my hand in his, Walker started to pull me back out to our friends before he looked over his shoulder at me and said my favorite six words. "I love you, my lucky Penny."

epilogue

Walker

5 Years Later

LOOKING through the house for my wife, I finally found her sitting outside on the balcony with a glass of wine in her hand and a serene smile on her face. "What are you doing out here?"

She looked back at me with a smile that stretched across her face. "Waiting for you to join me, so we can enjoy our first sunset set in our new house."

I sat down beside her on the love seat and took a sip of her wine before I brushed my lips to hers. "I would have been here sooner if I had known where you were."

303

"I knew you'd find me, eventually. I was wandering through the place, checking the rooms and furniture to make sure everything's all set up for when everyone arrives tomorrow, when I saw the sun starting to set. I thought since we're here to relax, I'd do just that."

Picking Pen up, I pulled her onto my lap so that her legs were draped over mine. "Who agreed to have guests after only being here a day? I think I want you all to myself for at least the next week or two."

Resting her cheek to my chest, Pen wrapped an arm around my waist and let out a contented sigh. "I think everyone will be busy with their significant other most of the time, and we'll have plenty of alone time while they're here." She nuzzled into my chest further. "I'm not sure I'm going to want to leave once the summer is over. It's so beautiful here."

"Someday, we'll call Greece our home full time. Until then, let's settle for a couple of months out of the year. Once we move here, you'll probably miss LA," I chuckled, knowing that was the understatement of the year. I wasn't sure how Pen could be so far away from Stella unless she planned to get her to buy a house here as well.

"I won't miss LA per se, but I will miss Stella and Lexie. I have a feeling once Lexie and Ryder see this place, they'll be wanting to come here instead of Rio every opportunity they get. This will be their new favorite spot;

then I'll just need to convince Stella and Remy to come here."

I wasn't so sure about that. I'd seen the pictures of the first time Ryder and Lexie had been to Rio, and even in the pictures, you could see their amazing chemistry. That place held something few others could. It was the same for us in this place. We acknowledged our love in Greece, and it was the spot where we got married.

Her fingers danced up my side and settled high on my chest. "Do you love it here?"

"I love anywhere you are, but yes, I love it here. If I didn't, I wouldn't have agreed to buy a second home in Oia when we could buy one anywhere in the world. This place is like living in a whole different world."

Pen sat up and rested her forehead to mine. For a long moment, she traced her fingertips over the plains of my face as she stared into my soul. The love I saw radiating back at me took my breath away.

"Did you ever picture your success ever being anything close to this big? For everyone to know your name and sing your songs?"

"No, but I also could never imagine finding someone who would make me settle down and never look at another woman again. If it wasn't for you, none of this would be possible."

Our second album, Corrupt Heartache, went platinum

after only two weeks of being released. Even though it felt like it damn near killed me, being away from Pen inspired some of the best music I've ever written. Cristiano firing Pen, and therefore us, was the next best thing. We had labels coming out of the woodwork for a chance to work with us. We took our time and found the label that we knew we'd be with forever. KWR was now our family. They made working with them the best experience, and they loved Pen as our manager.

Moving to straddle my legs, Pen fluffed out her skirt around us as she reached inside the waistband of my athletic shorts. "I love how you give me so much credit, but I think your sexy voice and the words you write have a lot to do with it."

"And I love what you have in mind right now." I pushed up into her hand as she started to slowly move it up and down my shaft.

"Before our guests arrive tomorrow, I figured we should christen the balcony and maybe a few more places. What do you say?" She nipped along my jaw and up to my ear. "Are you up for the challenge?"

"You know I'm always up for fucking you." Leaning my head back against the cushion, I slid my hands up her legs and under her skirt to find my wife without any panties on. Sliding my finger through her folds, I ran my tongue along the shell of her ear. "How long have you been bare under here?"

"Not for long. I took my thong off right before I came out here." She ran my cock through her slickness before lining me up at her entrance and slowly sank down.

"Fuck, Penny, you feel so damn good. This is my heaven. The place I want to be for the rest of my days." I pushed my hips up to meet hers, making my pelvis connect with her clit.

Putting her hands on my shoulders, Pen arched her back. Her face lit up by the fading sun that was slowly sinking below the horizon. She rose up and down and circled her hips as I ran my hand up her flowy top and cupped one breast and then the other. Pen arched further into me, riding me like there was no tomorrow.

Pulling her skirt up, I watched the way her pussy took every inch of me and sucked me back in time after time. I wasn't sure if there was anything more erotic than that sight.

"Walker," she whispered my name as her walls started to flutter around me. Her hands came to my shoulders as she started to chase her release. I knew exactly what she needed to bring her over the edge. Pushing the fabric of her shirt out of the way, I swirled my tongue around a tight pink bud as my thumb made slow circles on her clit. One touch and she started to clench around me until all there was, was her cunt milking my cock. Her fingers dug into my shoulders and back as Pen fell apart around me, and I quickly followed behind her.

Pen collapsed on top of me. Her forehead pressed to mine, and our panted breaths tangled together. "I think sex is better in Greece."

Kissing the side of her mouth, I chuckled. "I think I have to agree. Maybe we should move here permanently, and I can spend all my time inside of you."

Rolling her forehead on mine, she grinned. "How about you settle for the next..." she looked at the dwindling light and then back at me. "Twelve or so hours?"

"Hmmm," I stood up. Pen's legs wrapped around my waist. "Where do you think we should christen next?"

Turning to look inside the house, Pen tilted her head to the side. "How about the kitchen?"

"Wherever you want, Mrs. Pierce." I walked inside and directly to the kitchen, where I sat her on the kitchen island and spread her legs wide.

"You know it never gets old hearing you say that or seeing my ring on your finger." I lifted her left hand to my mouth and kissed the back of her hand.

Pulling her shirt over her head, Pen then lifted her skirt,

exposing herself to me once again. I ran my thumb over her slick lips, watching as my cum slowly seeped out.

Getting on my knees, I ran my nose up her inner thigh. "You're gorgeous everywhere. Have I told you that before?"

"Maybe a time or ten, but I never get tired of hearing it. The amazing person you are and way you look at me makes me love you more with each passing day."

"You make it easy when I'm around you. You bring out all the goodness in me as well as move me, heart, body, and soul."

Using her feet, she pushed my shorts down until they slipped and hit the floor. "When you say words like that, they take my breath away."

My mouth claimed hers in a searing kiss. When we finally pulled away, I ran my hand through her hair and tugged. "I only speak the truth of how you make me feel."

"If you're so inspired, maybe you should write a song about it," she giggled and then moaned as I ran the pad of my thumb over her sensitive nub.

"I have a feeling both you and this place will inspire many more songs to come. In the meantime, why don't you lean back and let me show you how much?"

For the rest of the night and early into the morning light, I showed Pen what words couldn't say. How not a day went by that I didn't thank the Greek gods Pen agreed to marry me. Hell, that an amazing woman like her even gave me a chance when she had so much to lose.

My muse. My soul. My everything.

WANT MORE of Walker and Pen? Get an exclusive epilogue when you sign up for my newsletter.

where it all began

This is where The Rocker started. I wrote this for something else and fell in love with Walker. I thought you might enjoy where it started and see where they are now.

epilogue 2
PEN

I stood to the side of the stage like the groupie I was and sang along to the music. Words I knew by heart. My body swayed to the beat in a practiced rhythm it knew all too well. The moment I heard the first note of Crimson Heat's debut song, I was an instant fan.

My body heated as I watched the lead singer, Walker Pierce, sing with his deep and raspy voice. It was an aphrodisiac to every red-blooded female on the planet— and quite a few men as well.

Glancing to my left, I watched as a woman with the biggest and fakest tits I'd ever seen threw her bra up on stage, barely missing the lead singer. He didn't miss a beat as a seasoned singer and kept going as if nothing had happened. I'd watched Crimson Heat rise from a barely known garage band into one of the biggest rock bands of the decade that sold out stadiums around the world only two years later.

I was in awe of their showmanship. At every concert I'd seen, and there had been hundreds, I noticed something else that made the band stand out amongst the others. No matter if it rained, snowed, was sweltering hot, or freezing cold at outdoor venues, they played like they were inside with the best conditions. Tonight, it was Kenton who looked more than a little worse for wear, probably hungover, but he still smashed his drums with the energy of a hummingbird. I'd seen Walker belt out lyrics while he had the flu, and no one ever knew he'd been sick until the article came out two days later.

Every time their concerts came to an end, I was sad yet exhilarated as the crowd went wild from their encore performance. Even with earplugs in, their screaming and clapping were almost deafening. I clapped and screamed along with them like I did at every concert I attended. There was nothing like seeing your favorite band up close in concert. It was a rush that I never wanted to end.

I watched as each guy went up to stand next to Walker, waved at the crowd, and bowed before they individually headed off stage. Each member eyed me as they moved past me and through the halls to their green room. Walker was the last to leave the stage. He gave one last flick of his wrist before he headed straight toward me.

Walker Pierce was raw masculinity in everything he did, even walking. He prowled toward me, his dark eyes piercing straight through me until he marched past me like I was nothing but a piece of gum beneath his shoe, and followed his band members into their room.

Slowly, I followed all the other groupie girls who hoped to have a shot with one or all the members of Crimson Heat tonight. I flashed my pass as needed to get by and waited patiently with everyone else in the hallway for one of the guys to open the door and let a few lucky people inside. I'd seen it done a dozen times before and watched hundreds walk away with broken hearts after not being picked. It always made me feel bad for the girls.

Tonight was special, and I had a feeling I would be one of the lucky ones. So did every other woman who was pushing up their boobs until they were near to bursting out of their skintight shirts, hiking up their skirts, and applying another layer of lip gloss to their overly plump lips. Pulling down the hem of my red halter top, I looked down at my leather skirt that was shorter than I was used to wearing. Seeing as my heels weren't as high, nor was my hair as perfectly coiffed as the rest of the women, made me second guess my chances for the night.

The door to their green room opened up, and out walked Cross, the bass guitarist. There was a burst of excitement as he went down the line of women on both sides of the hall and pointed at each deemed worthy or slutty enough to be let inside for the night. Cross passed me by and started back for the door when he turned to look over his shoulder and then pointed at me.

A smile stretched across my face as I took the few short steps to walk inside. Each member of the band was assessing the women they wanted as they made their way inside with hungry eyes and wrapped their arms around their shoulders once they picked their flavor for the night as they moved further into the small space.

Alcohol bottles of every type of liquor you could imagine filled one table with a line of people waiting to make their own drinks. I took this all in with new eyes. The eyes of being one of the chosen, even though none of the guys had picked me. Yet.

Eyes as dark as night met mine from across the room, making my breath catch. It was like I was locked in a tractor beam as Walker Pierce, the lead singer of Crimson Heat, sauntered toward me. We moved toward each other as if on instinct. The tips of his black combat boots met the toe of my red stilettos, showing how different we were from each other. He was all hard rocker, and I was a nobody desperate to be used by him. I took in his soaked plain, black t-shirt and dark-washed jeans that he filled out spectacularly. I'd never seen another man able to make clothes look as sexy as he did. Each article of clothing showcased his muscular build. Until that moment, I hadn't realized I hadn't taken a breath until his arm went around my waist and pulled me into the only unoccupied corner in the room.

With his large build, he blocked out the rest of the room, making it seem as if it was only the two of us. The sounds from everyone else faded away as his eyes raked over my skimpily clad body. From the way his pupils dilated and how his tongue darted out to lick his full bottom lip, I took it that he liked what he saw.

Leaning forward with his front flushed to mine, Walker ran his nose up the column of my neck and didn't stop until he met the shell of my ear. "What's your name?"

"Pen," I breathlessly answered.

"Pen?" he quirked a lone dark eyebrow and smirked. "What kind of name is that?"

Internally, my hackles rose, but I didn't let it show. Instead, I shrugged and then answered with my hands going to his chest and getting a feel of the steel muscles that were hidden behind the black fabric. "It's short for Penelope."

"Want a drink?" He tilted his head toward the bar on the other side of the room, reminding me we weren't alone. The rest of the band members were there pouring drinks for the women they'd chosen.

Curling one hand around the side of his neck, I pressed

my breasts further into his chest. "Not really, but I wouldn't mind having a drink of you."

Throwing his head back, Walker let out a raspy yet booming laugh, making everyone stop what they were doing and take notice. He was known to be serious and to barely ever crack a smile, so hearing his laughter was a prize for everyone to hear.

The second his laughter died down, the room went back to what they were previously doing, and the rush of their laughter and voices hit my ears.

Raising his large hand, Walker ran the pad of his thumb over my bottom lip. His eyes tracked his movement.

With his piercing gaze on my lips, my core clenched, and moisture started to slowly make its way down my thighs.

He hummed deep in his throat, eyes never leaving my ruby red lips. "Do you think your pretty little mouth can take all of my cock? Will you gag as I deep throat you and fuck your mouth until my cum dribbles down your chin?"

Without waiting for me to answer, Walker dipped his head low and took my mouth in a searing kiss. The moment our mouths collided, a zap of electricity jolted through me, making me gasp into his waiting mouth. He was rough, but it wasn't unexpected. Walker Pierce was a man who looked like he'd beat the shit out of you for no other reason than you looked at him wrong, but if you looked at him right, you were in for a night of rough and tantalizing sex.

His tongue delved into my mouth, tasting each inch of me. I moaned as I circled my tongue with his and was met with cinnamon. There was no fight. I let him dominate the kiss. The moment. The night.

Calloused hands slid up my thigh and then hitched my leg around his hip in one smooth move. Rough fingertips skated up my inner thigh and dug into the flesh of my ass as he cupped it roughly.

"I can smell how much you want me from here," he bit out, running his nose along my collarbone before he nipped at my exposed throat. "What do you say we take this somewhere a little more private?"

Without waiting for an answer, he clasped his fingers around my wrist and pulled me from the room. I jogged to keep up with his long strides down the hall and out into the cool night air, making my already aching feet throb painfully.

Walker navigated us through the lines of trucks, vans, and buses. Stopping in front of the door of the biggest and nicest bus from what I could tell in the dark, he banged on the door with his fist. A moment later, the door opened with a big burly guy standing at the entrance with a wry grin on his face.

Giving a chin lift, he moved out of the way as Walker

pulled me up the stairs and into the living area. "Yo, Walk. Do you want me to wait outside?"

"Nah, man, just don't interrupt us. No matter what you hear," Walker chuckled darkly, sending goosebumps across my entire body.

I met the eyes of the man in front of me as he laughed at Walker's comment. "Duly noted. Have fun."

"Always, man. Always," he answered before he turned and started to walk us away.

With my back to the front of the bus, his rough hands slid underneath the hem of my halter top and skidded up my taut stomach. I sucked in a breath when those large hands of his cupped my breasts and then pinched my nipples hard through the lacy fabric of my demi-cup bra. The way the lace scraped against my sensitive peaks made me wetter between my trembling legs. His hot breath on the column of my neck sent excited shivers down my spine as he kneaded and pulled at my breasts.

Being with Walker like this was a dream come true. It was my every fantasy come to life, and I couldn't believe I was finally here, alone on the bus with him and about to get the best ride of my life. Because I had no doubt tonight would be one epic fuck for the books.

Walker moved us to the back of the bus, my eyes taking in everything as we passed the small but nice leather furniture of the living area. It was nice and surprisingly clean, with four guys living in it. We passed by the bunks that were open with unmade beds and articles of personal items lining the insides of their area.

"It's been too long since I sunk my dick into a groupie slut's cunt. You want to know if the rumors are true? If my cock really is as big as they say?" He ground his erection into my back. If the hard mass pressed against me was any indication, I had a feeling the rumors were false. Walker was even bigger than anyone had ever let on. "I bet you're soaked for me, aren't you?"

Rubbing my stiff peak between his thumb and forefinger, he pinched and pulled, making me want to detonate from his fingers alone. "Answer me, groupie. Are you wet for me?"

"Yes," I moaned, arching up and into his touch.

Stepping inside the bedroom, he closed the door and slammed my front into it, pinning me against the door with his hard, lean body. My body quaked with want for him.

His harsh breath fanned my ear. "Do you like it rough?"

"Anything you want," I panted like an animal in heat. I was desperate to feel him inside of me.

"Good, because I'm going to fuck you so hard, you'll never be able to forget me," he gritted out before he bit down on the shell of my ear.

Keeping me in place with his weight against me,

Walker roughly pushed my leather skirt up my thighs and around my waist. The cool air from the bus hit my bare pussy. I was hot, like I'd been lost in the desert for days with the sun beating down on me.

"You are a little slut, aren't you? Were you planning on one of us ramming our dick into you?" He slapped my pussy, making my whole-body quake.

My only answer was a shake of my head. I couldn't speak as unexpected pleasure shot through my body.

"Liar," he husked in my ear.

His hands moved up my sides, taking my halter top along with them until it was pushed up over my breasts. He wasted no time in pulling down the cups and exposing my heaving tits to the cool air and the warm flesh of his hands.

I turned to look at him over my shoulder, wanting to see how he feasted on what he was doing to me but was stopped short when he fisted my hair in his hand, yanking me back to look forward at the black door I was pushed up against.

He stepped back but kept his firm hold on my hair. Instantly, I missed the heat of his body and wanted to feel him pressed back against me until the end of time. "This is my show, and you're just along for the ride. Now, do as I say and spread your legs."

Doing as he commanded, I stepped out and waited for my next instruction.

"Further," he growled.

I widened my stance and waited.

It was quiet for a moment, and then I heard the clomp of his boots as they hit the floor, the zipper of his jeans going down, and then the rustle of clothing as it was removed. Desperately, I wanted to turn around and see Walker in all his naked glory, but I knew I'd be punished. It didn't matter that the room was barely lit, with the only light filtering in through the tinted windows. I wanted to rake my eyes over him and his sexy as sin tattoos that graced his upper torso and arms.

He kept quiet as he moved around the room, and then, in an instant, his front pushed into my back. His skin to mine felt like touching the sun. With that touch alone, my vision blanked, and my skin seared at his touch.

Shifting a minute amount, he plunged two fingers deep into my core and pumped twice. "You're fucking soaked for me, slut. Are you a dirty girl? Do you get off on being fucked by rock stars?" Pulling his fingers out, he ran the silky wetness around my clit, drew slow circles, and then repeated the act again and again.

"Only you," I moaned into his touch. The rough pads of his fingers were a sharp contrast to my silky heat, making me want more. Grinding down on his fingers, he pulled his hand away and slapped my ass. Hard.

"Remember, this is my show. Now be a good girl and

get on your knees for me. I want to paint your pretty lips with my come."

Doing as he asked, I kneeled before him. Placing my hands on his thick thighs, I opened my mouth and ran my tongue up and then down his shaft before I took him all the way in and down my throat. The hair on his thighs pricked my breasts, turning me on all the more.

"You're the perfect little slut, aren't you?" he groaned, deep in his throat. The tips of his fingers gripped the sides of my head as he fucked my mouth without reprieve. My core pulsed with want. Sliding one hand down his leg, I went to relieve myself when he slapped it away. "Did I give you permission to touch yourself? I'm the only one who's going to bring you pleasure tonight."

Angry, he thrust into my mouth faster and harder. Without warning, he shot his hot load down my throat and filled my mouth as he pulled out and let one last shot go off down my neck and chest.

"Back on your feet," he demanded.

I'd never had a man be so demanding in the bedroom, and it was strangely exhilarating. I couldn't help but want more.

The moment I got to my feet, Walker went down on his own knees and threw one of my legs over his shoulder. One lick of his smooth tongue, and I was seconds away from detonating. Slipping two fingers in my slick channel, he thrust them with deep strokes and curled them on the way out, hitting me in the right spot, nearly making my leg go out from underneath me. Walker wrapped an arm around my waist to keep me steady as he removed his now lubed fingers and ran them around my hole. He let one tip start to slide in but halted his movements.

Stopping his ministrations, he lifted his head and asked. "Have you ever had a man here?"

"Never." I barely got the word out before his finger was inside of me, and he was fucking me in the ass while his tongue swirled around my clit and then sucked it hard into his mouth.

My entire body clenched and shook as pleasure shot through me, making me barely able to hold on to reality. My fingers threaded through his thick black hair and held on for dear life as he kept fucking me with his fingers and tongue. Throwing my head back, I screamed his name over and over again until my throat was hoarse.

Once my orgasm had subsided, he rubbed the rough pad of his thumb over my overly sensitive nub, and I whimpered out his name.

He let out a low chuckle as he stood to his full height and moved into me. The sound of a condom wrapper crinkled, and then he was backing me into the door. "Turn around and assume the position."

My legs wobbled as I turned on my heels. "I'm not sure I can stand after that. Can we use the bed?"

"Sorry, I don't let groupie sluts in my bed." He ran the tip of his cock through my wet folds and leaned in. "You can leave if you don't want this."

Reaching around, I placed him at my entrance and pushed back until I took in every inch of him. If I hadn't been so wet, I would have been full and stretched almost to the point of pain.

"That's what I thought," he said darkly.

Banding one arm around my middle, Walker held me upright as he fucked me hard. I knew I'd be sore for a week once we were done, but I didn't care. It was worth it.

His other hand went to my throat and turned my head so he could lick along my face as he pumped into me fast and hard. With each brutal thrust, a moan slipped from my lips as I pushed back into his long and thick cock.

I panted with my arms thrown against the door to hold myself up as Walker tightened his hold on my throat. My walls started to pulse.

"Not yet. You don't get to come until I say."

Luckily, I could feel him swell inside me and knew he wouldn't be able to hold on for much longer.

The arm around my waist loosened, and his hand moved between my legs. "Let go now," he ordered as he pinched my clit.

My body ignited, falling back against his slick chest. My arm went around his neck and held on as stars lit up my vision in the otherwise dark room.

When I finally came down, Walker had me in his arms. I nuzzled into his neck as my eyelids started to droop from all the amazing sex.

He kissed my temple as he laid me down and wrapped me in his arms. Our bodies molded together as we tangled our limbs.

"That was fun. I like it when we play," I said, letting my eyes slowly close.

"It was our best one yet." He pulled me in tighter to his body.

Kissing the side of his neck, I murmured. "I love you."

"I love you, too. Happy anniversary, baby," he murmured in my ear. "I can't wait to see what you come up with next year."

Did you enjoy THE ROCKER? If so, please consider leaving a review on Goodreads, Amazon, or BookBub. Reviews mean the world to authors especially to authors who are starting out. You can help get your favorite books into the hands of new readers.

I'd appreciate your help in spreading the word and it will only take a moment to leave a quick review. It can be as short or as long as you like. Your review could be the deciding factor or whether or not someone else buys my book.

http://bit.ly/HarlowLayneNL

acknowledgments

My family- your support means so much. Thank you for all of your encouragement and giving me the time to do what makes me happy.

To **my girls**: QB Tyler , Carmel Rhodes, Kelsey Cheyenne, Erica Marselas. I love each and every one of you. Thank you for all of your support.

Amanda: Thank you for talking me through when I didn't know where this story would go and being my cheerleader.

Thank you **Bex** for making my story into a book.

To all my **author friends**, you know who you are. Thank you for accepting me and making me feel welcome in this amazing community.

Lovers thank you for always being there day or night in my group.

To each and every **reader**, **reviewer**, and **blogger** - I would be nowhere without you. Thank you for taking a chance on an unknown author.

about harlow

Indie Author. Romance Writer. Reader. Mom. Wife. Dog Lover. Addicted to all things Happily Ever After and Amazon.

Harlow Layne is a hopeless romantic who writes sweet and sexy alpha males who will make you swoon.

Harlow wrote fanfiction for years before she decided to try her hand at a story that had been swimming in her head for years.

When Harlow's not writing you'll find her online shopping on Amazon, Facebook, or Instagram, reading, or hanging out with her family and two dogs.

also by harlow layne

Fairlane Series - Small Town Romance

Hollywood Redemption - Single Parent, Suspense

Unsteady in Love - Second Chance, Military

Kiss Me - Holiday, Insta-Love

Fearless to Love - Insta- Love

Love is Blind Series- Reverse Age Gap Romance

Intern - Office Romance

The Model - Workplace Romance

The Bosun - Military, First Responder

The Doctor - Surprise pregnancy

The Rocker - Rockstar

Hidden Oasis Series

Walk the Line - First Responder, Suspense

Secret Admirer - Damsel in Distress, Opposites Attract, Suspense

Til Death Do Us Part - Accidental Marriage, Insta-love

My Ex Girlfriend's Brother - MM, age gap

MM Romances

You Make It Easy -Second Chance

My Ex Girlfriend's Brother - MM - November 8

Chance Encounter - Enemies-to-Lovers

Collaborations

Basic Chemistry - Student/Teacher

Forever - Student/Teacher, Curvy girl, enemies-to-lovers

Worlds

Cocky Suit - RomCom, Office, Interracial

Risk - Forbidden, Sports

Affinity - Part of the Fairlane Series - Accidental Marriage, Enemies-to-Lovers

Until Delilah - Single Parent, Romantic Suspense with The Model tie-in